To ALAN

PLAY BALL!

Fuzzy Baseball

John Steven Gurney

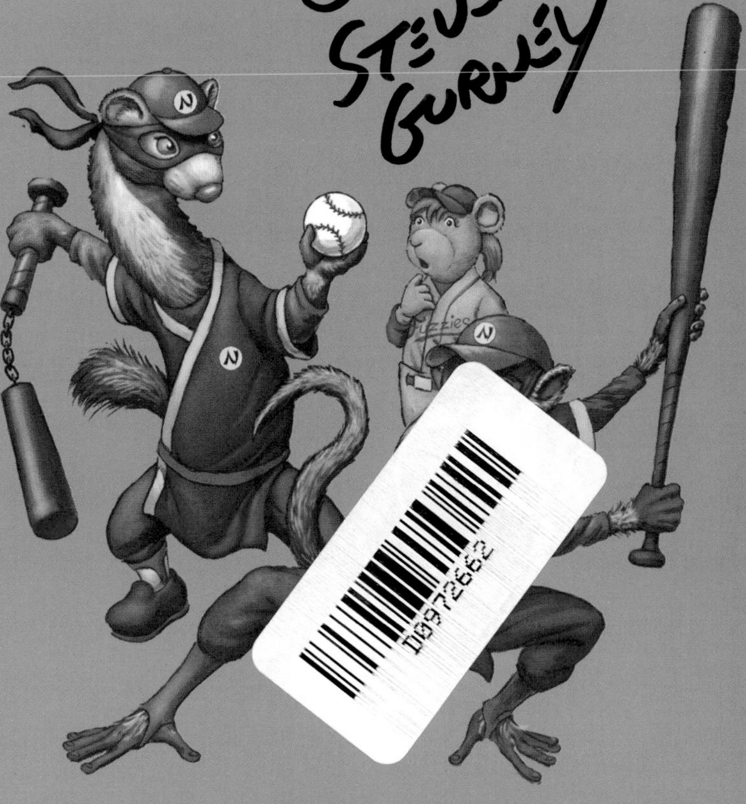
Fuzzies

John Steven Gurney

PAPERCUTZ

MORE GREAT GRAPHIC NOVELS FROM PAPERCUTZ

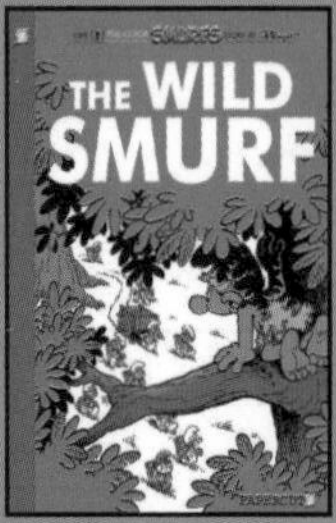
THE WILD SMURF

THE SMURFS #21

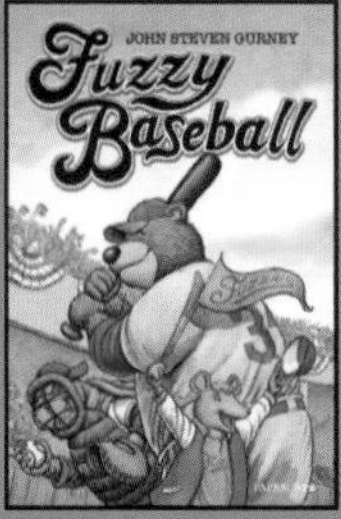
JOHN STEVEN GURNEY
Fuzzy Baseball

FUZZY BASEBALL #1

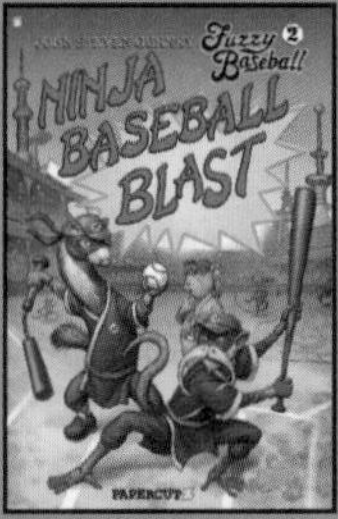
Fuzzy Baseball 2
NINJA BASEBALL BLAST

FUZZY BASEBALL #2

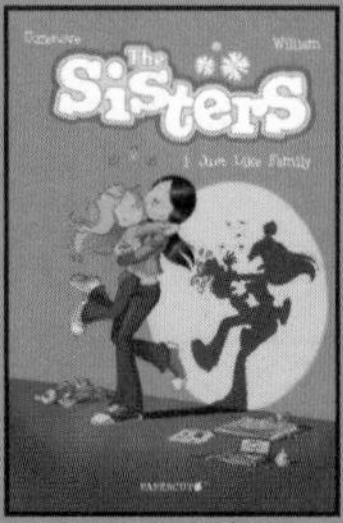
The Sisters

THE SISTERS #1

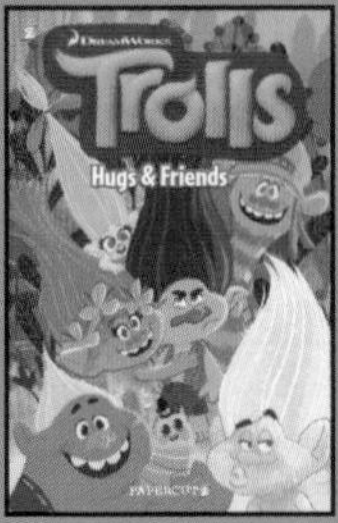
Trolls
Hugs & Friends

TROLLS #1

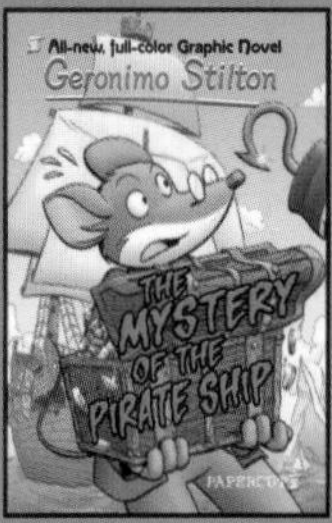
All-new, full-color Graphic Novel
Geronimo Stilton
THE MYSTERY OF THE PIRATE SHIP

GERONIMO STILTON #17

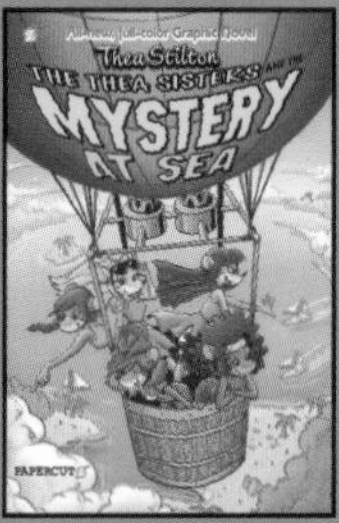
Thea Stilton
MYSTERY AT SEA

THEA STILTON #6

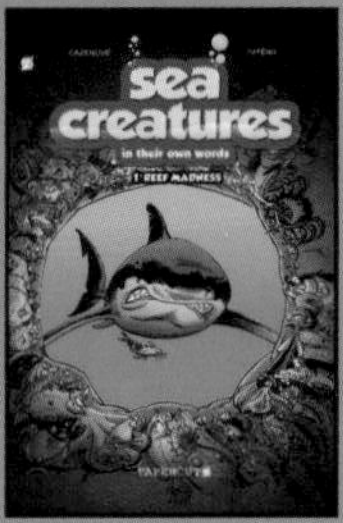
sea creatures
in their own words
REEF MADNESS

SEA CREATURES #1

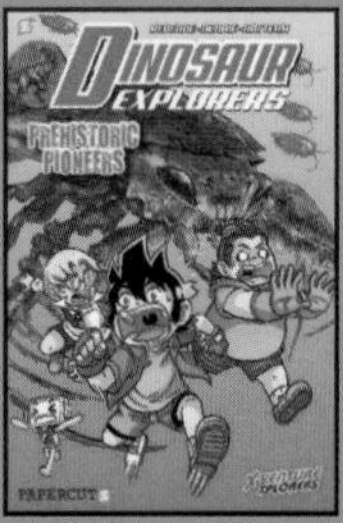
DINOSAUR EXPLORERS
PREHISTORIC PIONEERS

DINOSAUR EXPLORERS #1

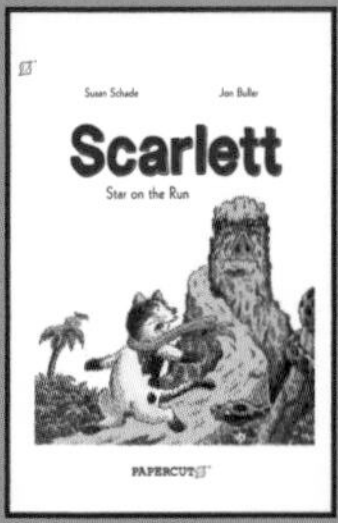
Susan Schade
Jon Buller
Scarlett
Star on the Run
PAPERCUTZ

SCARLETT

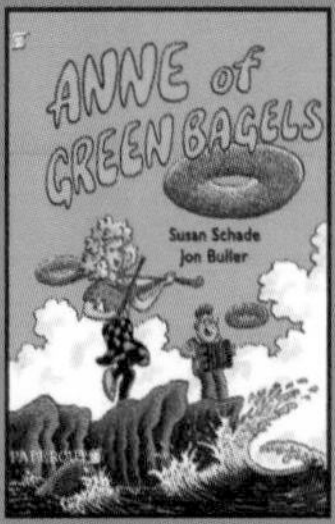
ANNE of GREEN BAGELS
Susan Schade
Jon Buller

ANNE OF GREEN BAGELS #1

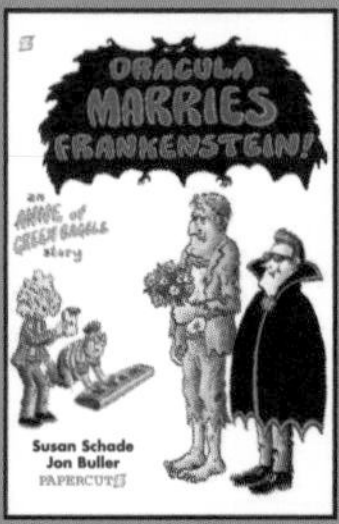
DRACULA MARRIES FRANKENSTEIN!
Susan Schade
Jon Buller
PAPERCUTZ

DRACULA MARRIES FRANKENSTEIN!

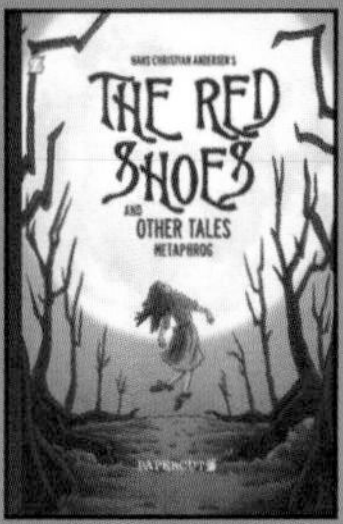
HANS CHRISTIAN ANDERSEN'S
THE RED SHOES
AND OTHER TALES
METAPHROG

THE RED SHOES

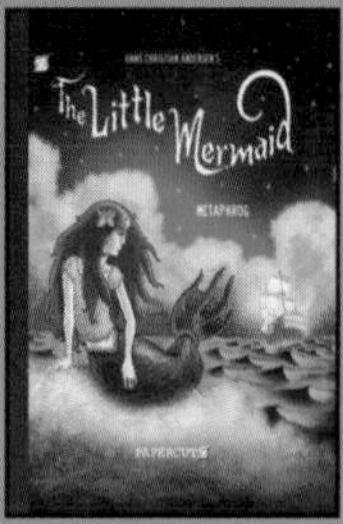
The Little Mermaid
METAPHROG

THE LITTLE MERMAID

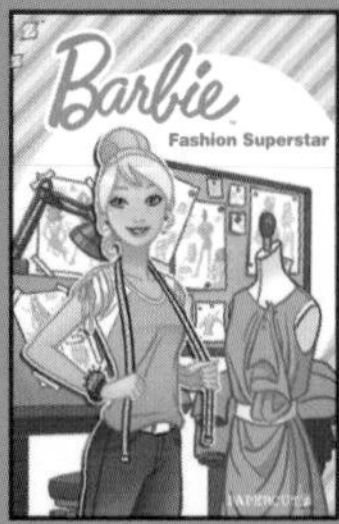
Barbie
Fashion Superstar

BARBIE #1

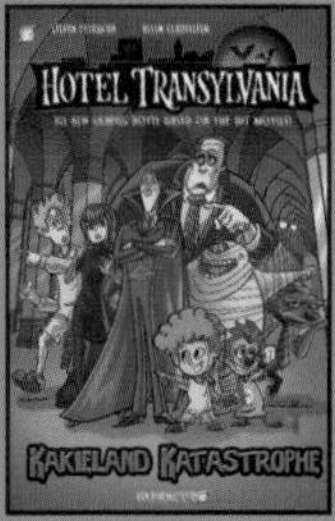
HOTEL TRANSYLVANIA
KAKIELAND KATASTROPHE

HOTEL TRANSYLVANIA #1

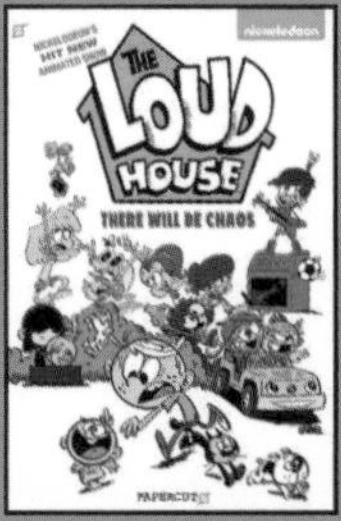
nickelodeon
THE LOUD HOUSE
THERE WILL BE CHAOS

THE LOUD HOUSE #1

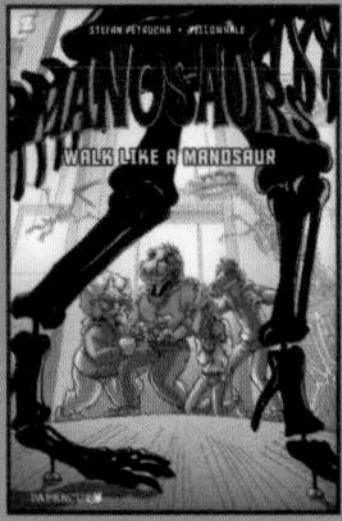
MANOSAURS
WALK LIKE A MANOSAUR

MANOSAURS #1

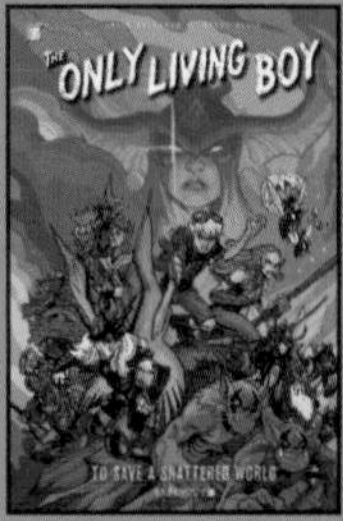
THE ONLY LIVING BOY
TO SAVE A SHATTERED WORLD

THE ONLY LIVING BOY #5

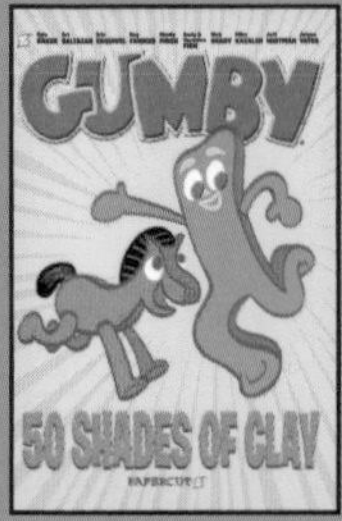
GUMBY
50 SHADES OF CLAY

GUMBY #1

SEE MORE AT PAPERCUTZ.COM

Fuzzy Baseball

2

NINJA BASEBALL BLAST

John Steven Gurney

PAPERCUTZ
New York

Fuzzy Baseball #2

"Ninja Baseball Blast"

Created by JOHN STEVEN GURNEY

MANOSAUR MARTIN—Production

KARR ANTUNES—Editorial Intern

JEFF WHITMAN—Managing Editor

JIM SALICRUP
Editor-in-Chief

Hardcover ISBN: 978-1-5458-0008-9

Paperback ISBN: 978-1-5458-0366-0

Printed in India
May 2019
Papercutz books may be purchased for business or promotional use.
For information on bulk purchases please contact
Macmillan Corporate and Premium Sales Department at
(800) 221-795 x5442.

Distributed by Macmillan
First printing

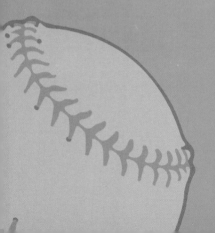

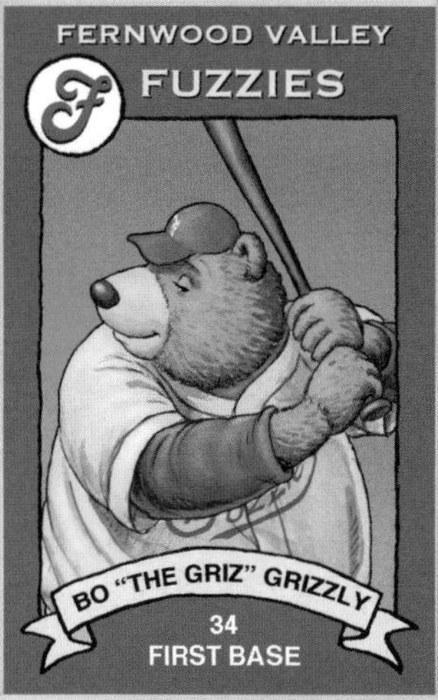
FERNWOOD VALLEY
FUZZIES
BO "THE GRIZ" GRIZZLY
34
FIRST BASE

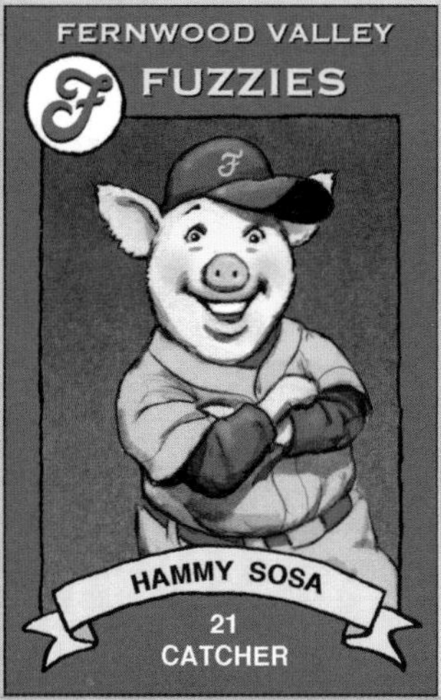
FERNWOOD VALLEY
FUZZIES
HAMMY SOSA
21
CATCHER

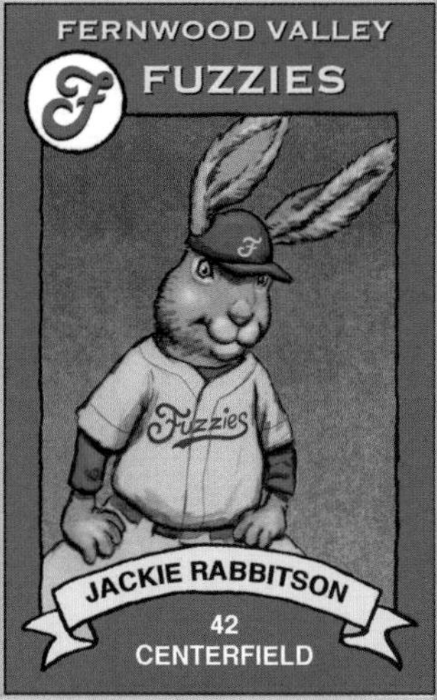
FERNWOOD VALLEY
FUZZIES
Fuzzies
JACKIE RABBITSON
42
CENTERFIELD

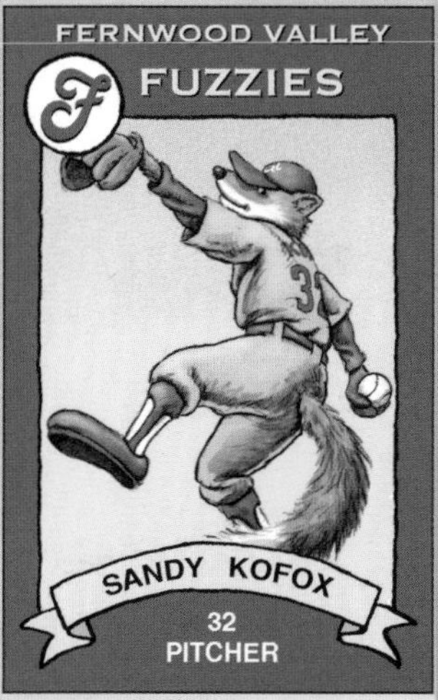
FERNWOOD VALLEY
FUZZIES
SANDY KOFOX
32
PITCHER

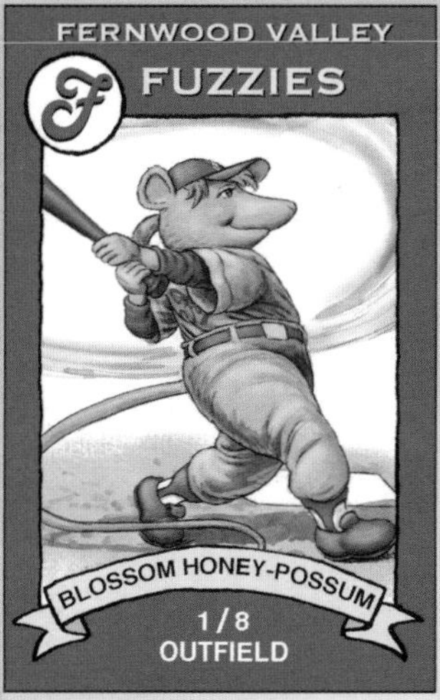
FERNWOOD VALLEY
FUZZIES
BLOSSOM HONEY-POSSUM
1/8
OUTFIELD

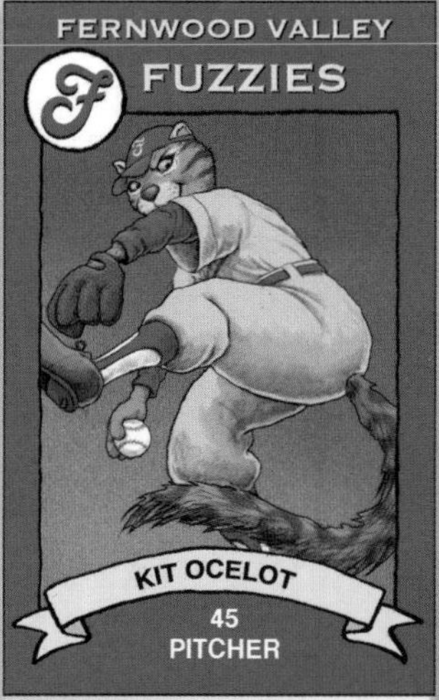
FERNWOOD VALLEY
FUZZIES
KIT OCELOT
45
PITCHER

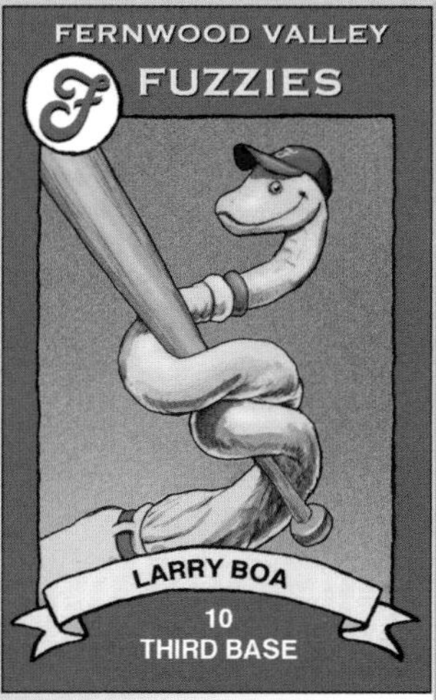
FERNWOOD VALLEY
FUZZIES
LARRY BOA
10
THIRD BASE

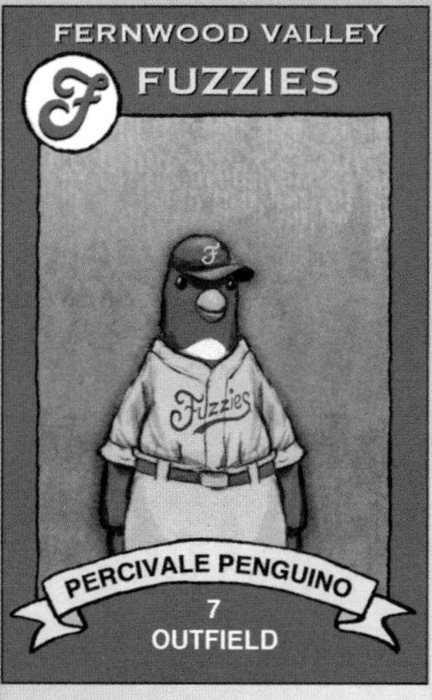
FERNWOOD VALLEY
FUZZIES
Fuzzies
PERCIVALE PENGUINO
7
OUTFIELD

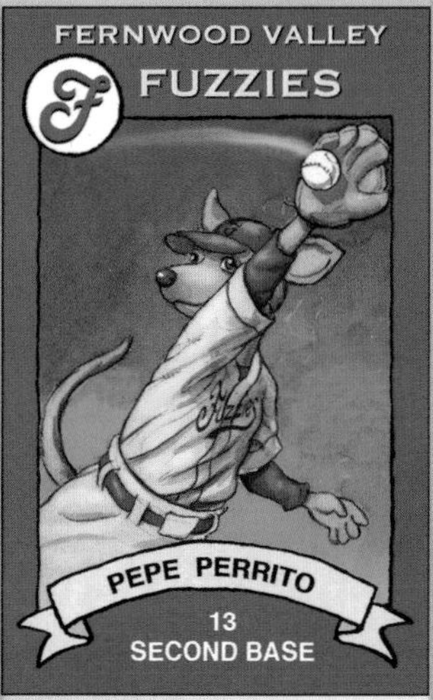
FERNWOOD VALLEY
FUZZIES
PEPE PERRITO
13
SECOND BASE

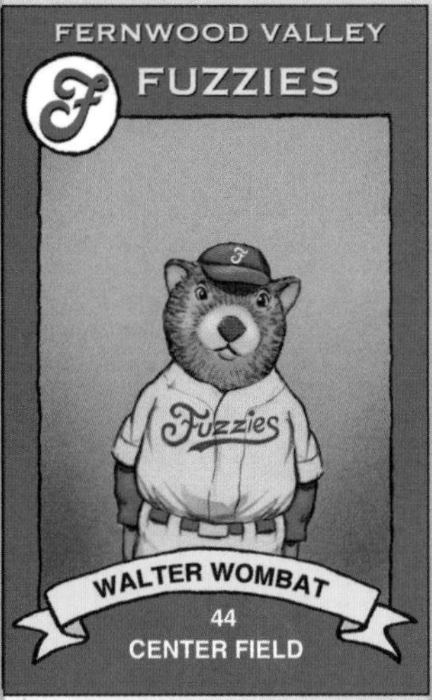
FERNWOOD VALLEY
FUZZIES
Fuzzies
WALTER WOMBAT
44
CENTER FIELD

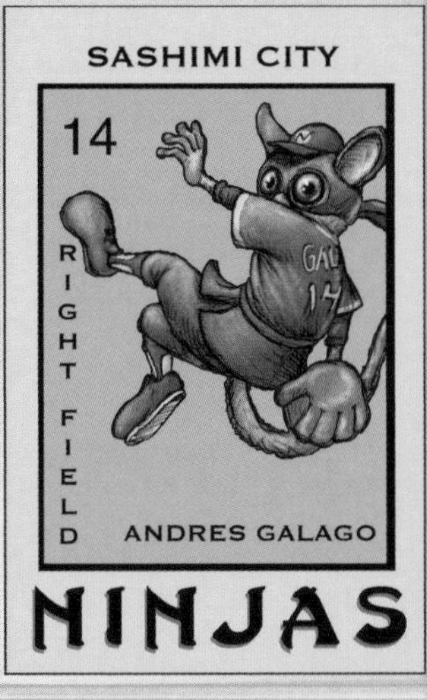
SASHIMI CITY
14
RIGHT FIELD
ANDRES GALAGO
NINJAS

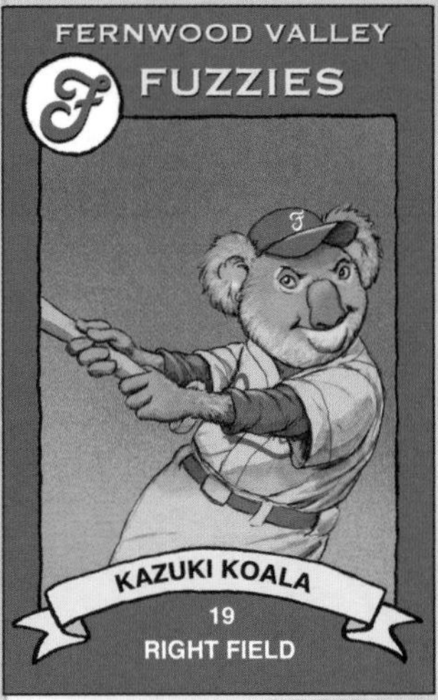
FERNWOOD VALLEY
FUZZIES
KAZUKI KOALA
19
RIGHT FIELD

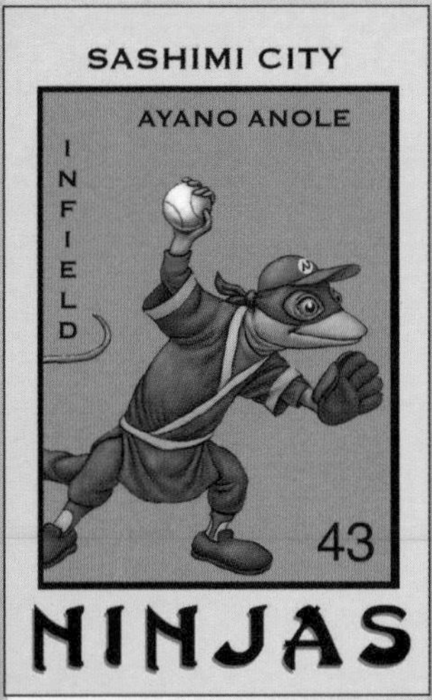
SASHIMI CITY
AYANO ANOLE
INFIELD
43
NINJAS

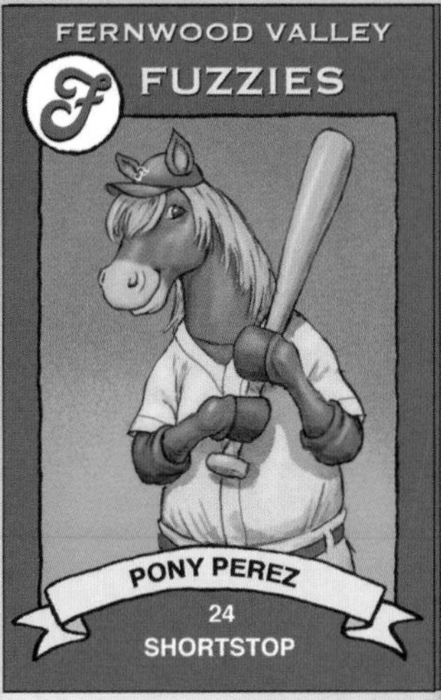
FERNWOOD VALLEY
FUZZIES
PONY PEREZ
24
SHORTSTOP

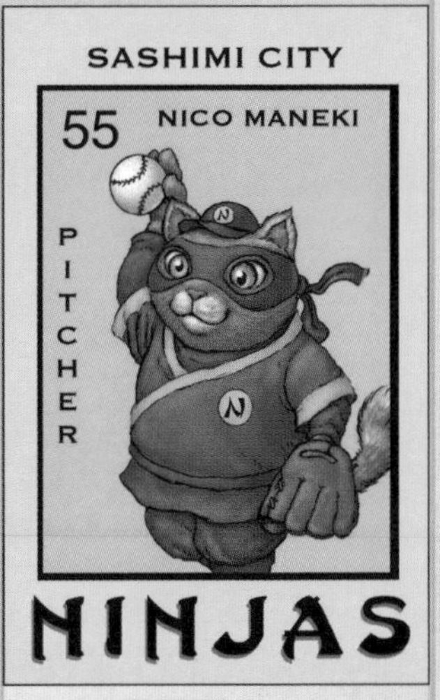
SASHIMI CITY
55
NICO MANEKI
PITCHER
NINJAS

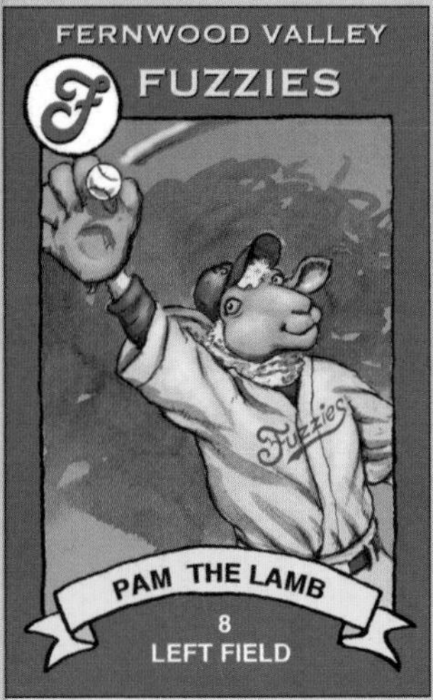
FERNWOOD VALLEY
FUZZIES
Fuzzies
PAM THE LAMB
8
LEFT FIELD

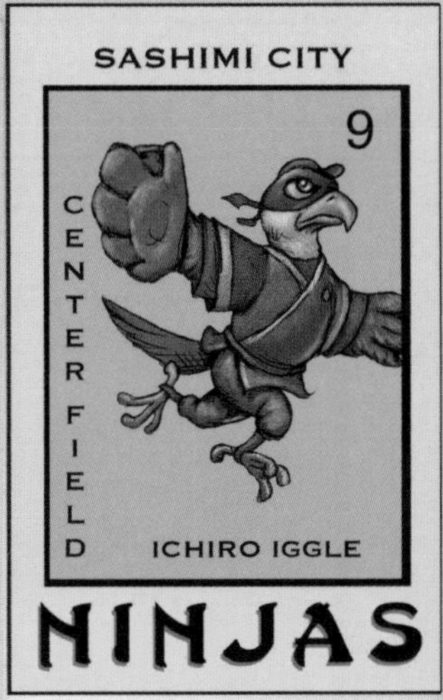
SASHIMI CITY
9
CENTER FIELD
ICHIRO IGGLE
NINJAS

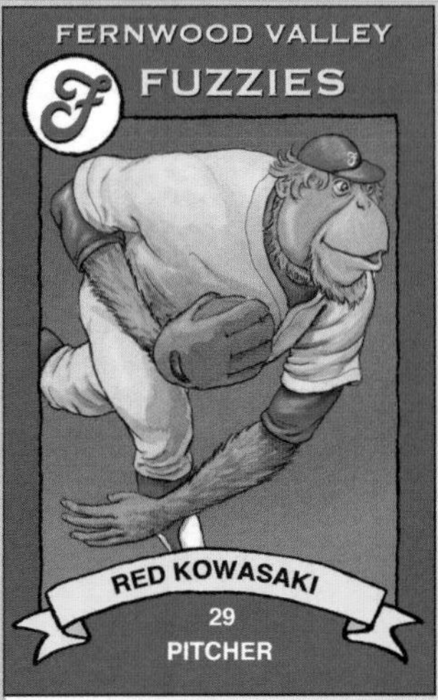
FERNWOOD VALLEY
FUZZIES
RED KOWASAKI
29
PITCHER

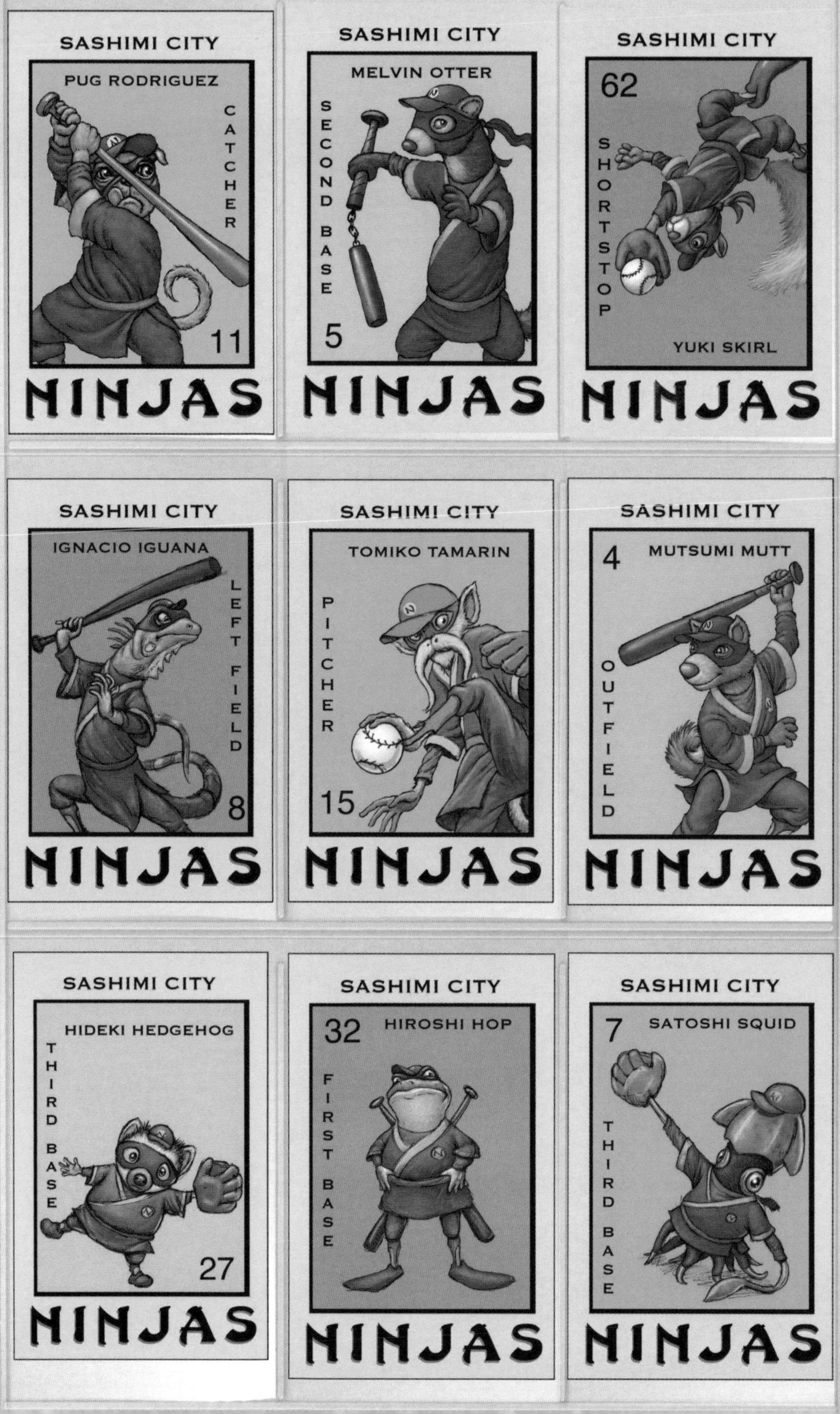
SASHIMI CITY
PUG RODRIGUEZ
CATCHER
11
NINJAS
SASHIMI CITY
MELVIN OTTER
SECOND BASE
5
NINJAS
SASHIMI CITY
62
SHORTSTOP
YUKI SKIRL
NINJAS
SASHIMI CITY
IGNACIO IGUANA
LEFT FIELD
8
NINJAS
SASHIMI CITY
TOMIKO TAMARIN
PITCHER
15
NINJAS
SASHIMI CITY
4
MUTSUMI MUTT
OUTFIELD
NINJAS
SASHIMI CITY
HIDEKI HEDGEHOG
THIRD BASE
27
NINJAS
SASHIMI CITY
32
HIROSHI HOP
FIRST BASE
NINJAS
SASHIMI CITY
7
SATOSHI SQUID
THIRD BASE
NINJAS

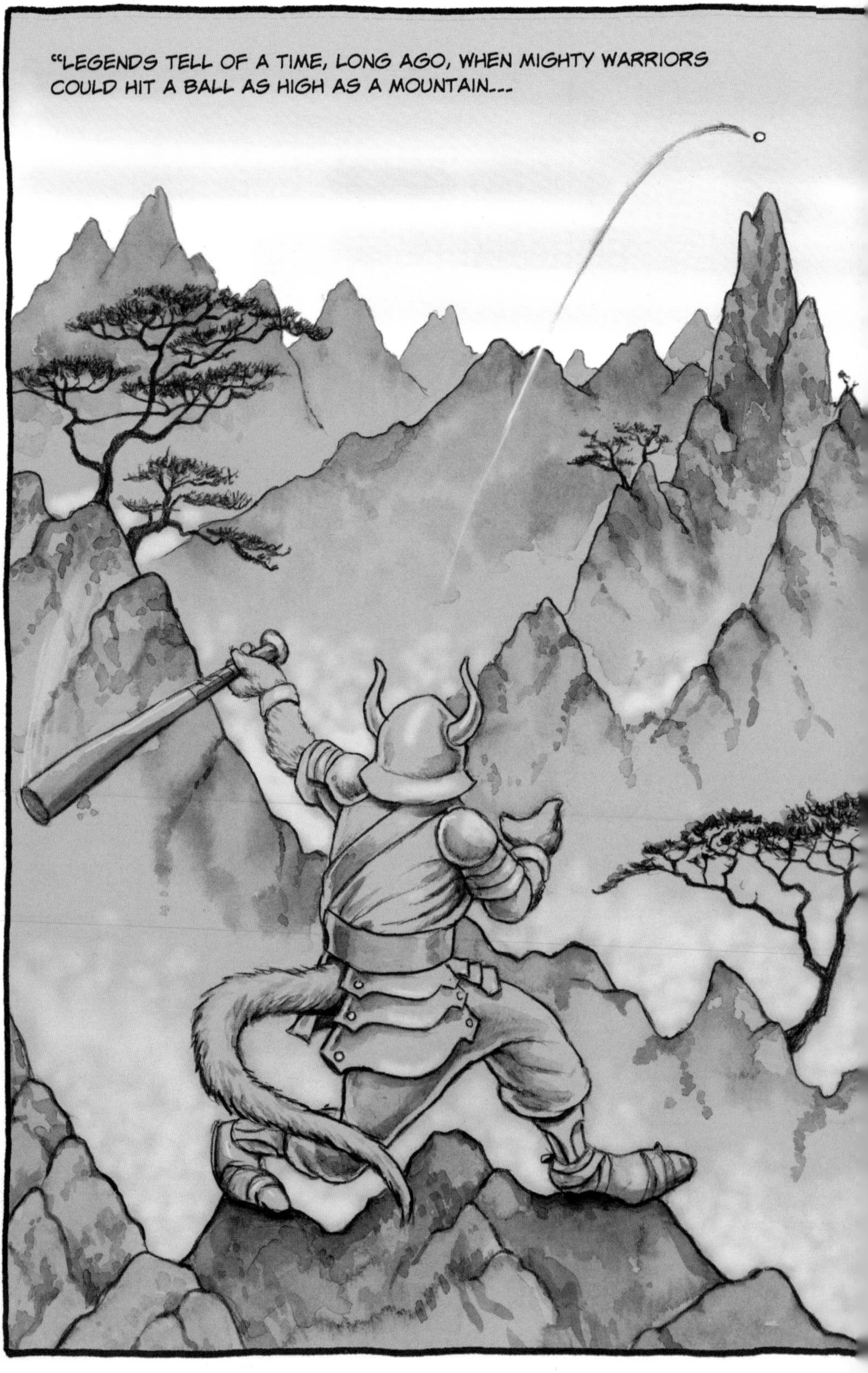
"LEGENDS TELL OF A TIME, LONG AGO, WHEN MIGHTY WARRIORS COULD HIT A BALL AS HIGH AS A MOUNTAIN...

"THEY COULD RUN SWIFTER THAN A FLYING ARROW....

"THE BALLS THEY THREW WOULD ZIGZAG THROUGH THE AIR LIKE LIGHTENING BOLTS.

"THEY WERE MASTERS OF STEALTH AND COULD STEAL A BASE IN THE BLINK OF AN EYE...."

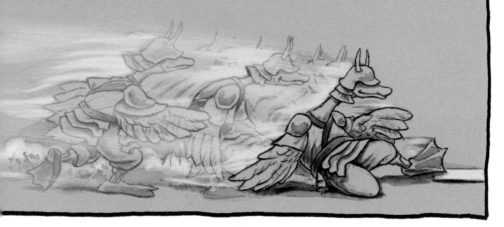

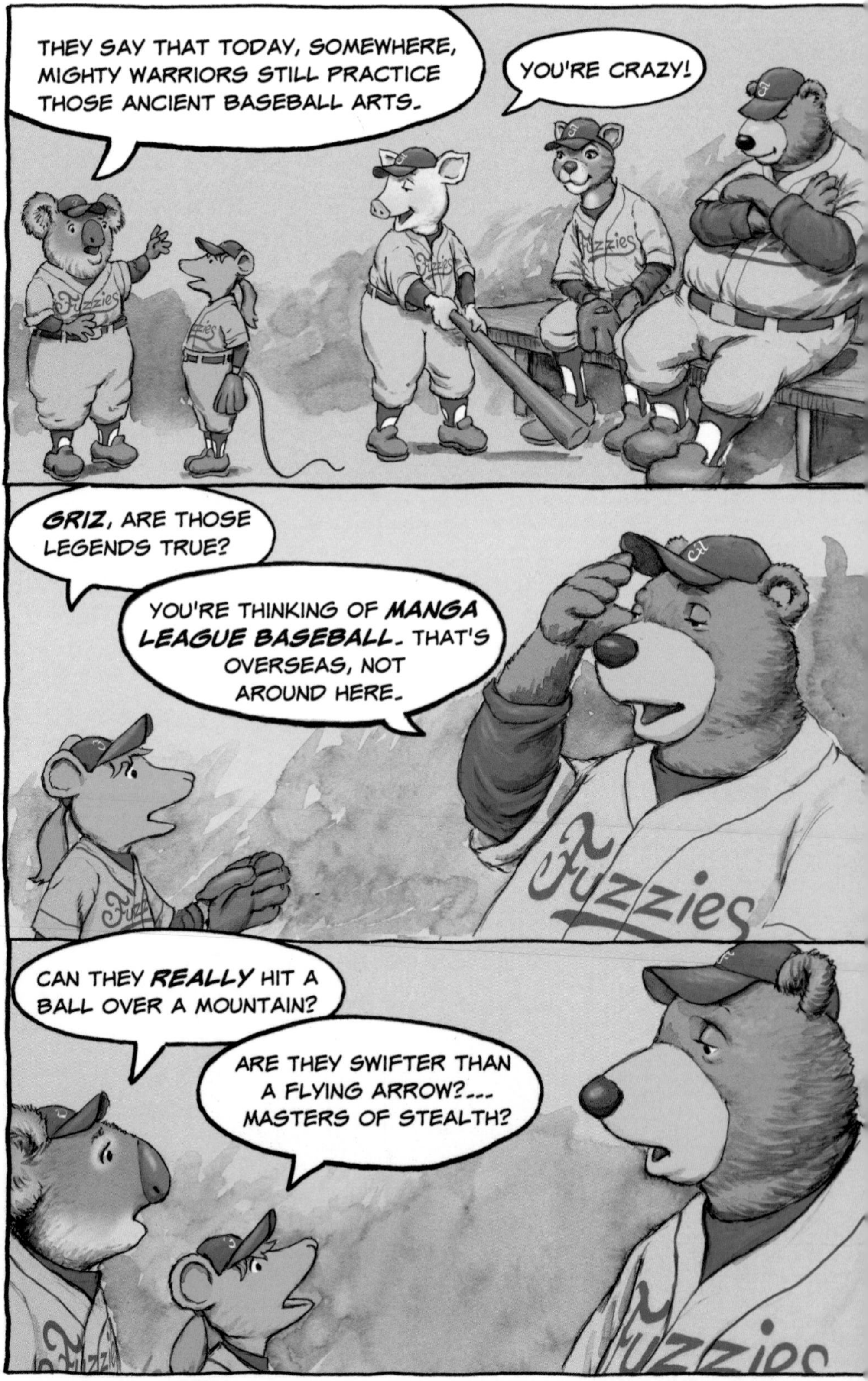
THEY SAY THAT TODAY, SOMEWHERE, MIGHTY WARRIORS STILL PRACTICE THOSE ANCIENT BASEBALL ARTS.
YOU'RE CRAZY!
GRIZ, ARE THOSE LEGENDS TRUE?
YOU'RE THINKING OF MANGA LEAGUE BASEBALL. THAT'S OVERSEAS, NOT AROUND HERE.
CAN THEY REALLY HIT A BALL OVER A MOUNTAIN?
ARE THEY SWIFTER THAN A FLYING ARROW?... MASTERS OF STEALTH?

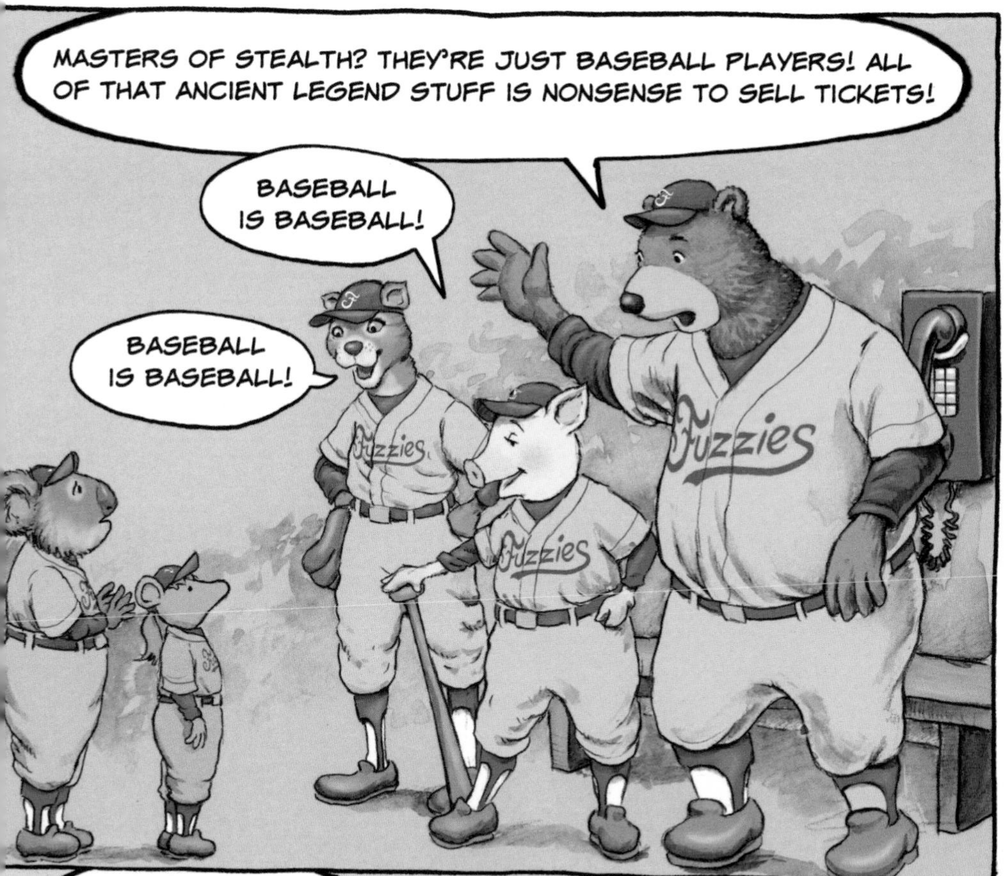
MASTERS OF STEALTH? THEY'RE JUST BASEBALL PLAYERS! ALL OF THAT ANCIENT LEGEND STUFF IS NONSENSE TO SELL TICKETS!
BASEBALL IS BASEBALL!
BASEBALL IS BASEBALL!

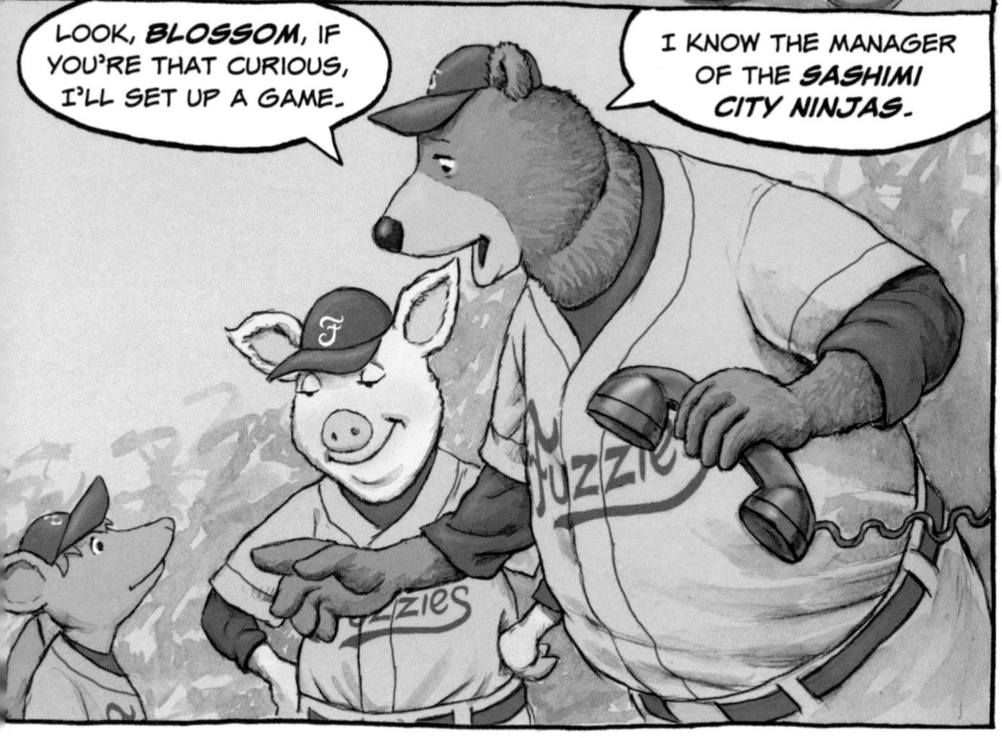
LOOK, **BLOSSOM**, IF YOU'RE THAT CURIOUS, I'LL SET UP A GAME.
I KNOW THE MANAGER OF THE ***SASHIMI CITY NINJAS***.

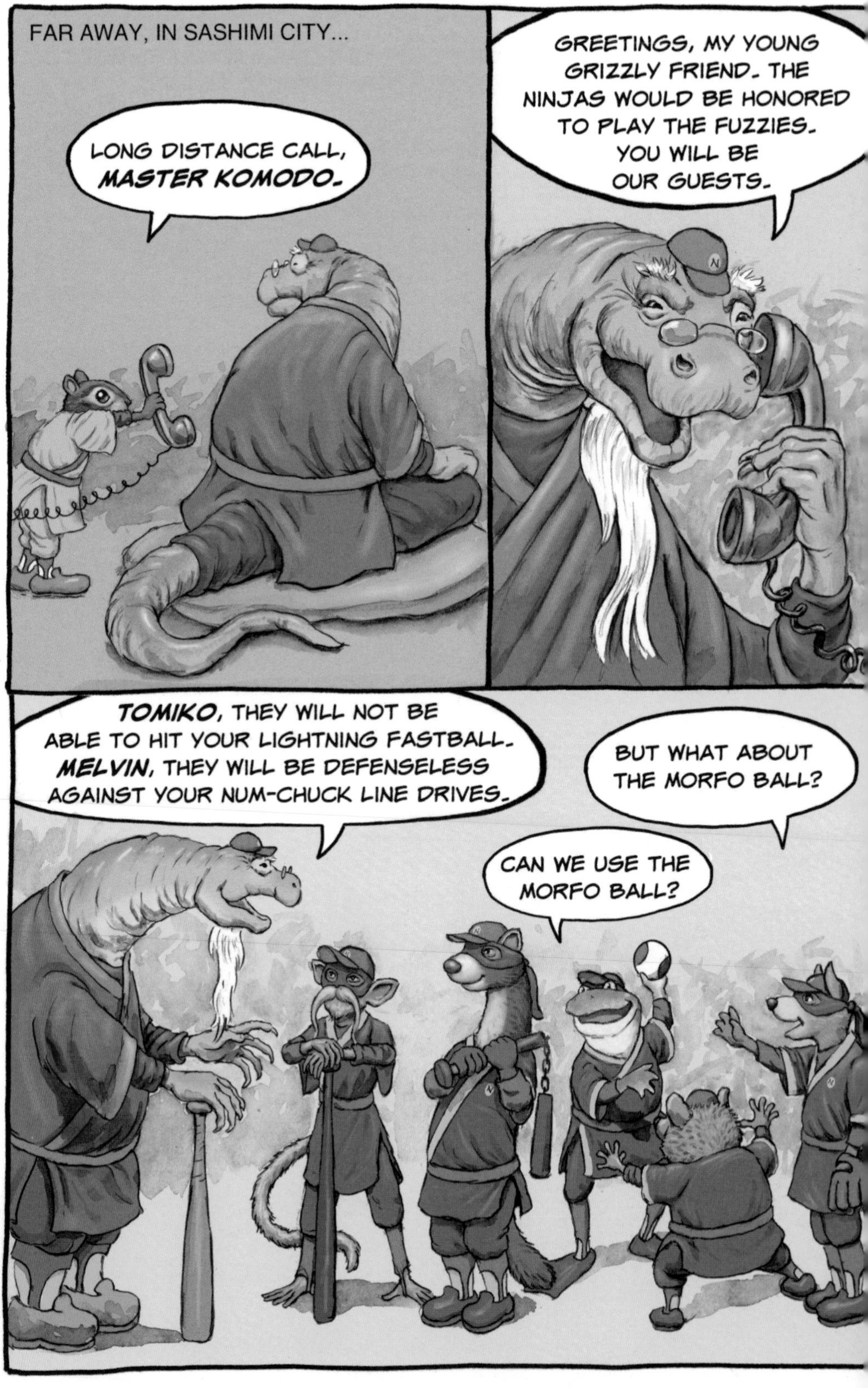

FAR AWAY, IN SASHIMI CITY...
LONG DISTANCE CALL, MASTER KOMODO.
GREETINGS, MY YOUNG GRIZZLY FRIEND. THE NINJAS WOULD BE HONORED TO PLAY THE FUZZIES. YOU WILL BE OUR GUESTS.
TOMIKO, THEY WILL NOT BE ABLE TO HIT YOUR LIGHTNING FASTBALL. MELVIN, THEY WILL BE DEFENSELESS AGAINST YOUR NUM-CHUCK LINE DRIVES.
BUT WHAT ABOUT THE MORFO BALL?
CAN WE USE THE MORFO BALL?

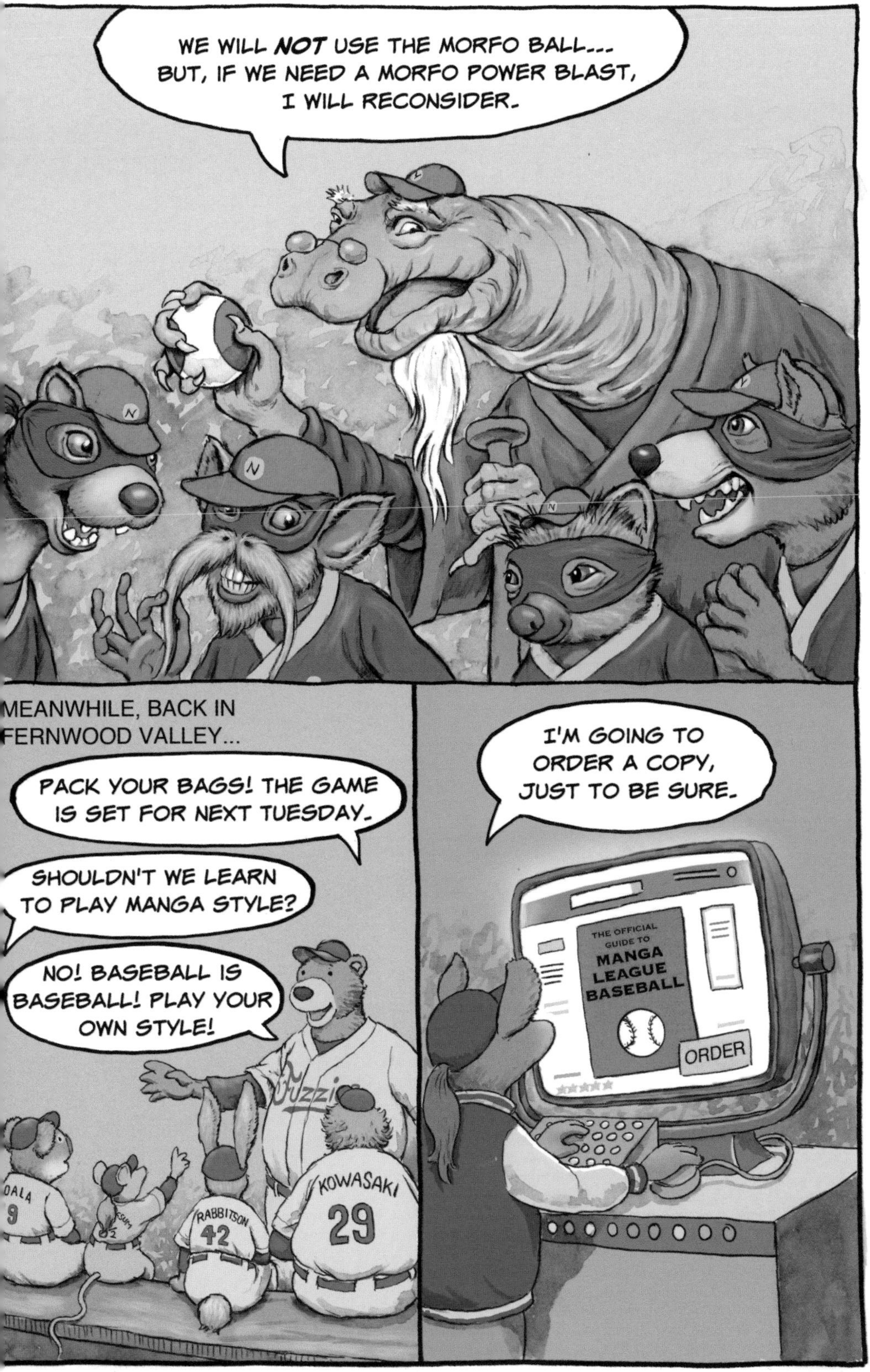
WE WILL ***NOT*** USE THE MORFO BALL... BUT, IF WE NEED A MORFO POWER BLAST, I WILL RECONSIDER.
MEANWHILE, BACK IN FERNWOOD VALLEY...
PACK YOUR BAGS! THE GAME IS SET FOR NEXT TUESDAY.
SHOULDN'T WE LEARN TO PLAY MANGA STYLE?
NO! BASEBALL IS BASEBALL! PLAY YOUR OWN STYLE!
RABBITSON 42
KOWASAKI 29
I'M GOING TO ORDER A COPY, JUST TO BE SURE.
THE OFFICIAL GUIDE TO MANGA LEAGUE BASEBALL
ORDER

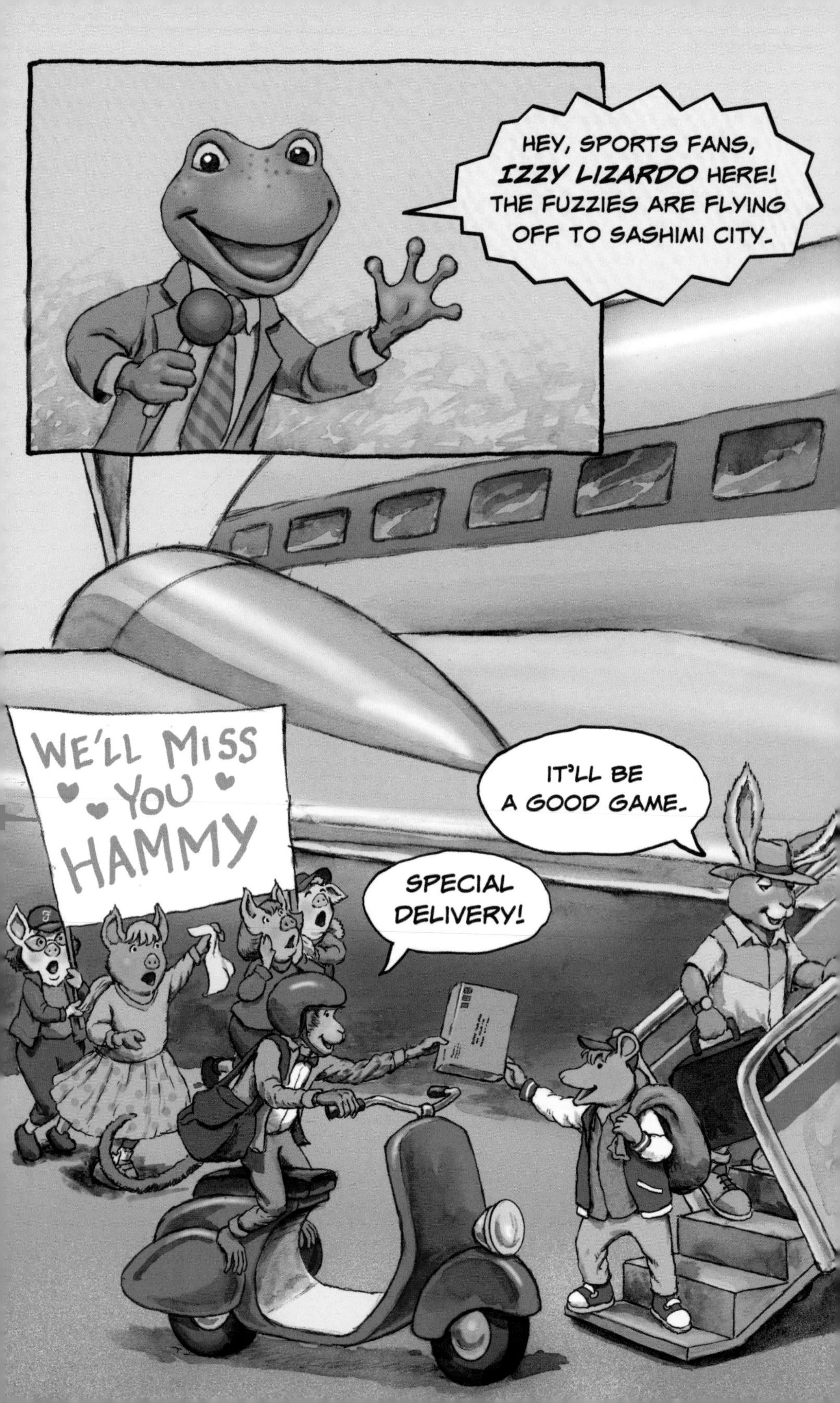
HEY, SPORTS FANS, IZZY LIZARDO HERE! THE FUZZIES ARE FLYING OFF TO SASHIMI CITY.
WE'LL MISS YOU HAMMY
IT'LL BE A GOOD GAME.
SPECIAL DELIVERY!

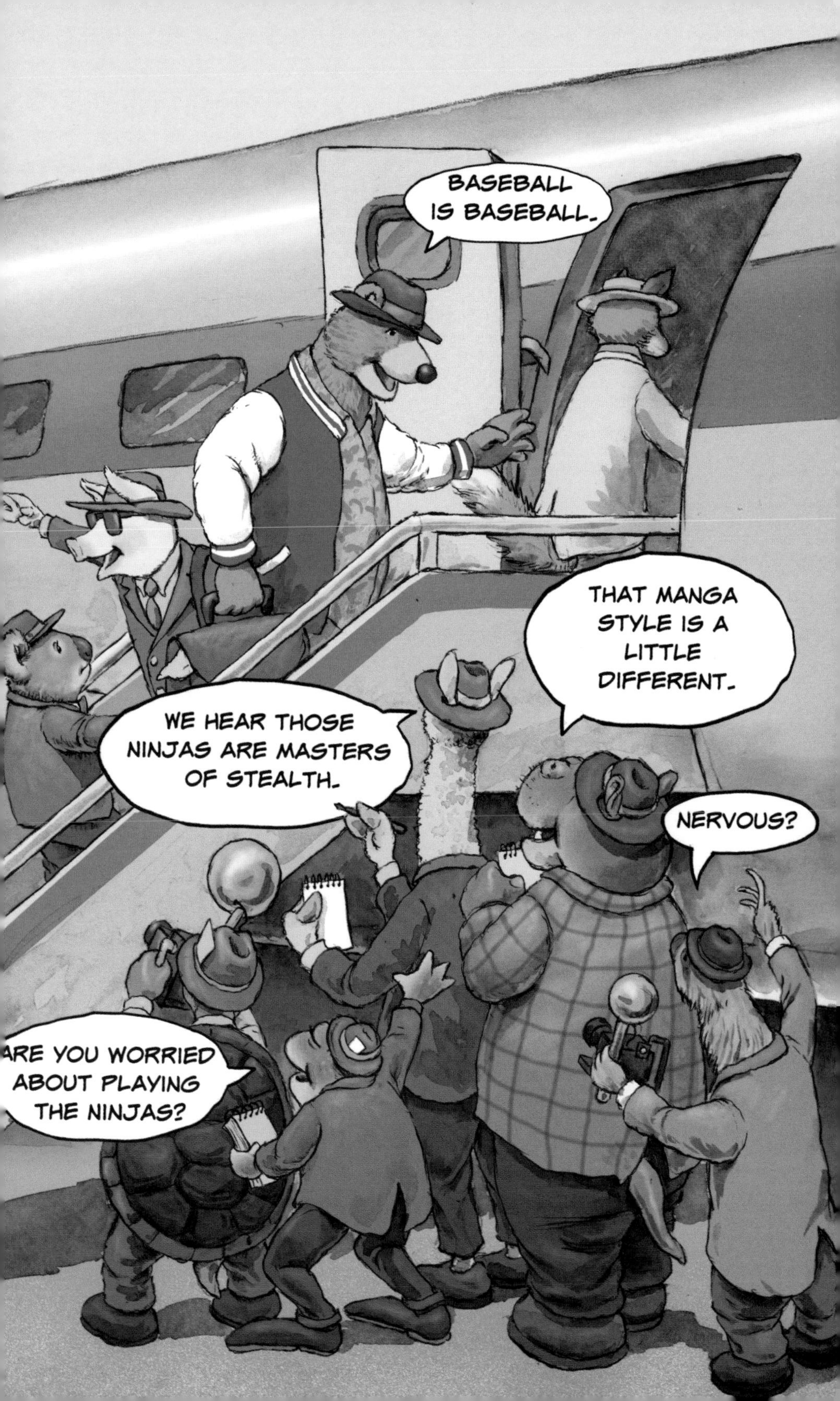
BASEBALL IS BASEBALL.
THAT MANGA STYLE IS A LITTLE DIFFERENT.
WE HEAR THOSE NINJAS ARE MASTERS OF STEALTH.
NERVOUS?
ARE YOU WORRIED ABOUT PLAYING THE NINJAS?

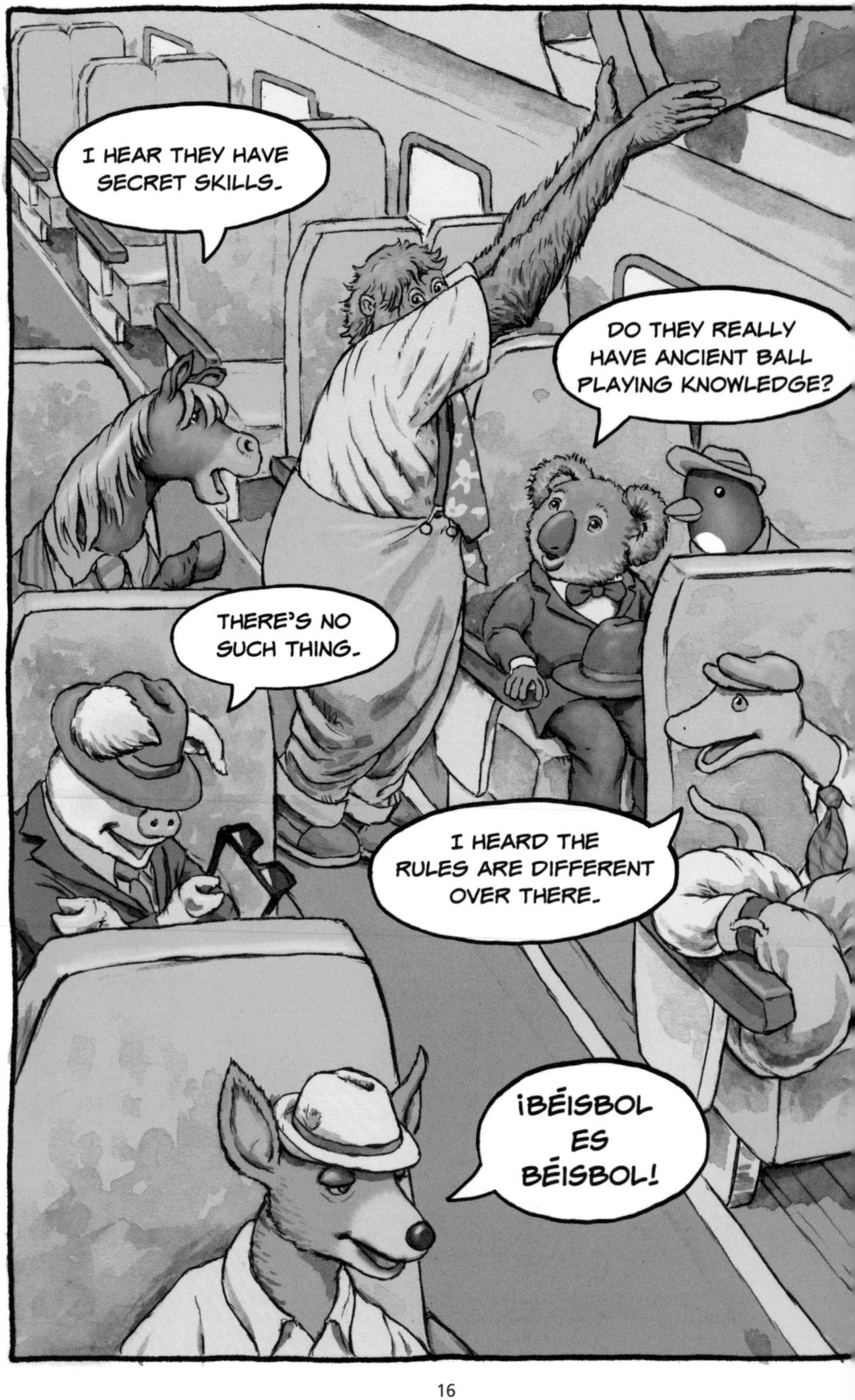
I HEAR THEY HAVE SECRET SKILLS.
DO THEY REALLY HAVE ANCIENT BALL PLAYING KNOWLEDGE?
THERE'S NO SUCH THING.
I HEARD THE RULES ARE DIFFERENT OVER THERE.
¡BÉISBOL ES BÉISBOL!

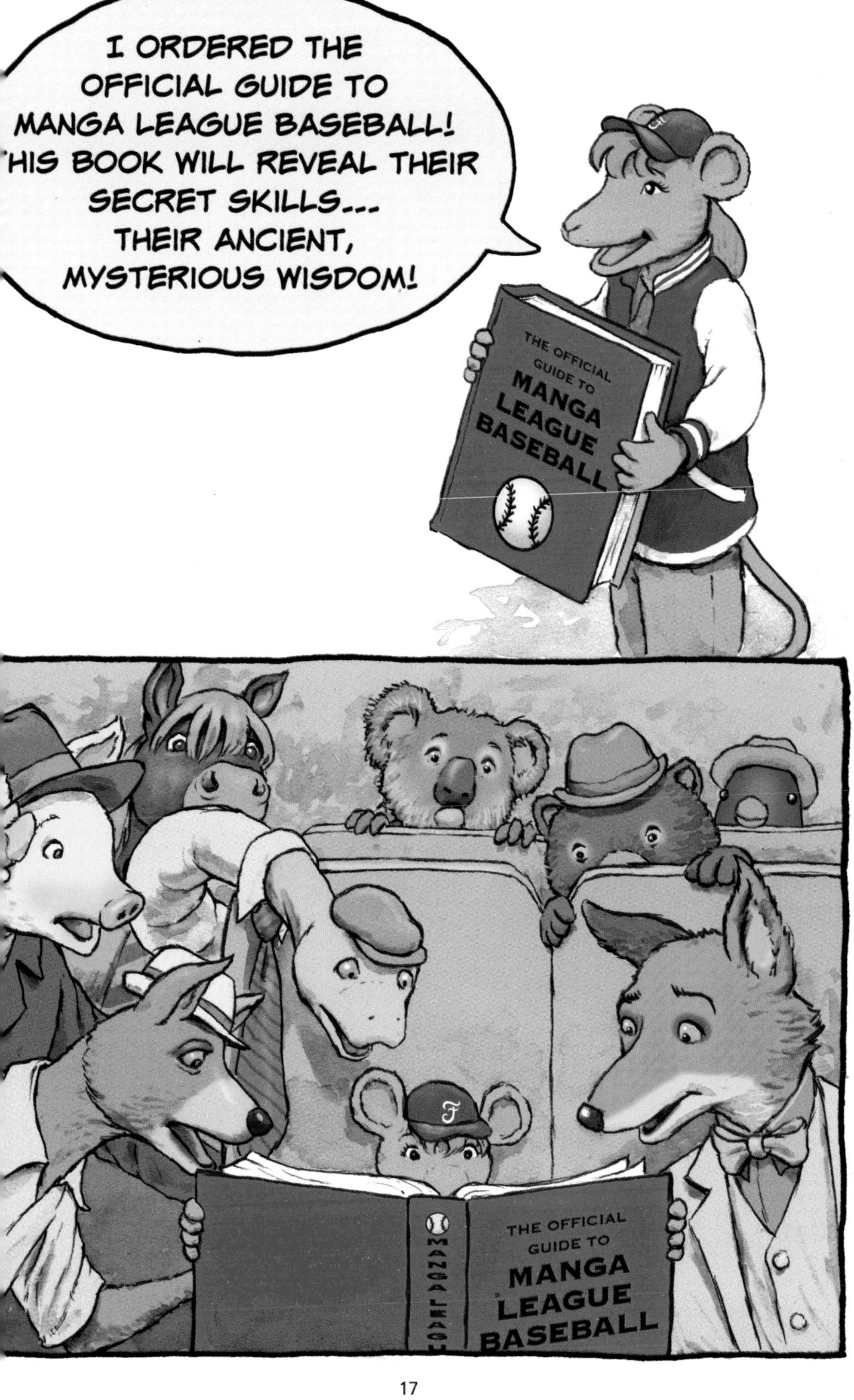
I ORDERED THE OFFICIAL GUIDE TO MANGA LEAGUE BASEBALL! HIS BOOK WILL REVEAL THEIR SECRET SKILLS... THEIR ANCIENT, MYSTERIOUS WISDOM!
THE OFFICIAL GUIDE TO MANGA LEAGUE BASEBALL
MANGA LEAGU
THE OFFICIAL GUIDE TO MANGA LEAGUE BASEBALL

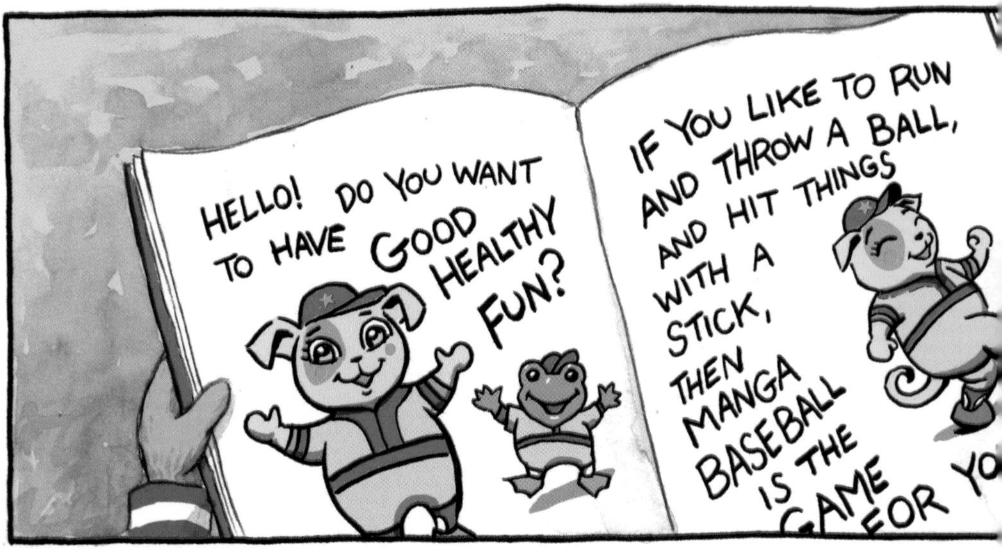
HELLO! DO YOU WANT TO HAVE GOOD HEALTHY FUN?
IF YOU LIKE TO RUN AND THROW A BALL, AND HIT THINGS WITH A STICK, THEN MANGA BASEBALL IS THE GAME FOR YO

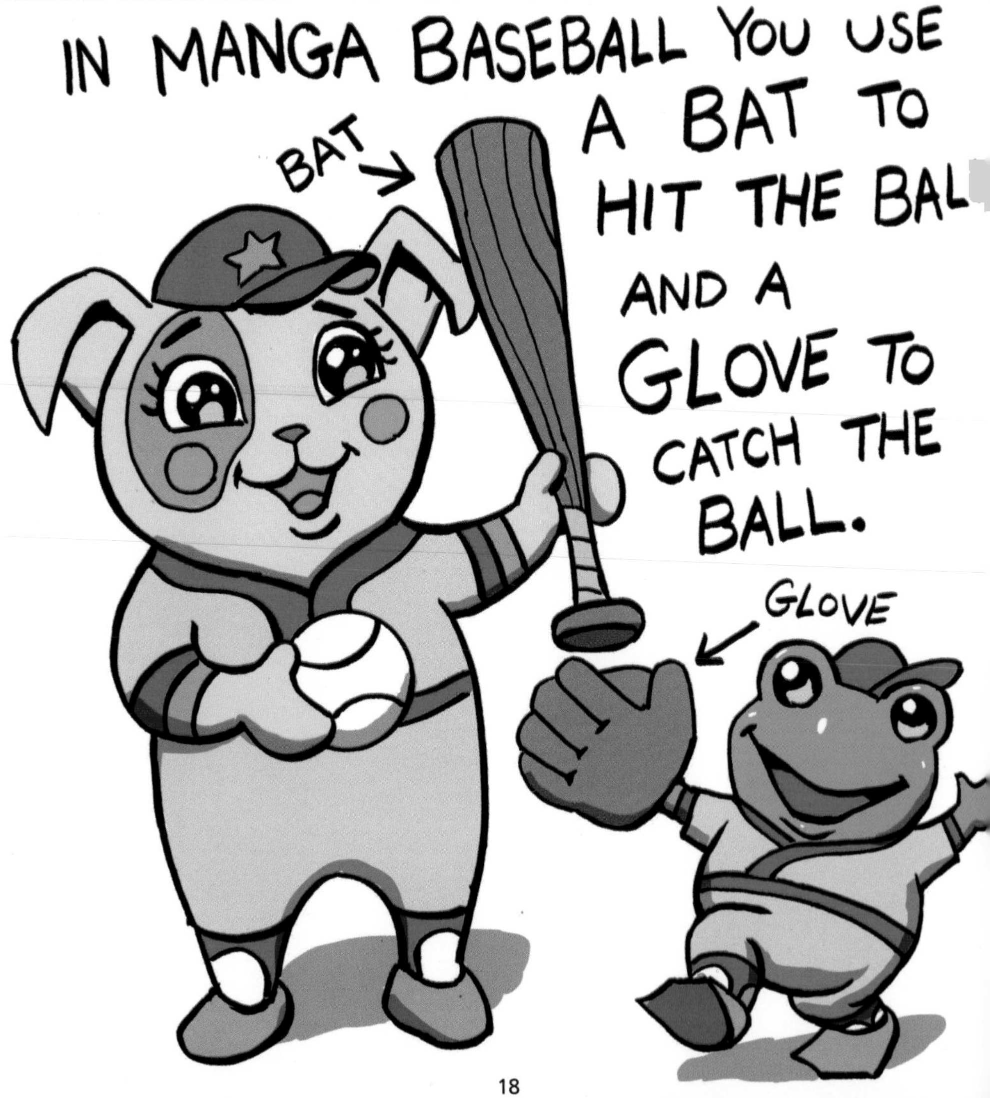
IN MANGA BASEBALL YOU USE A BAT TO HIT THE BAL
AND A GLOVE TO CATCH THE BALL.
BAT
GLOVE

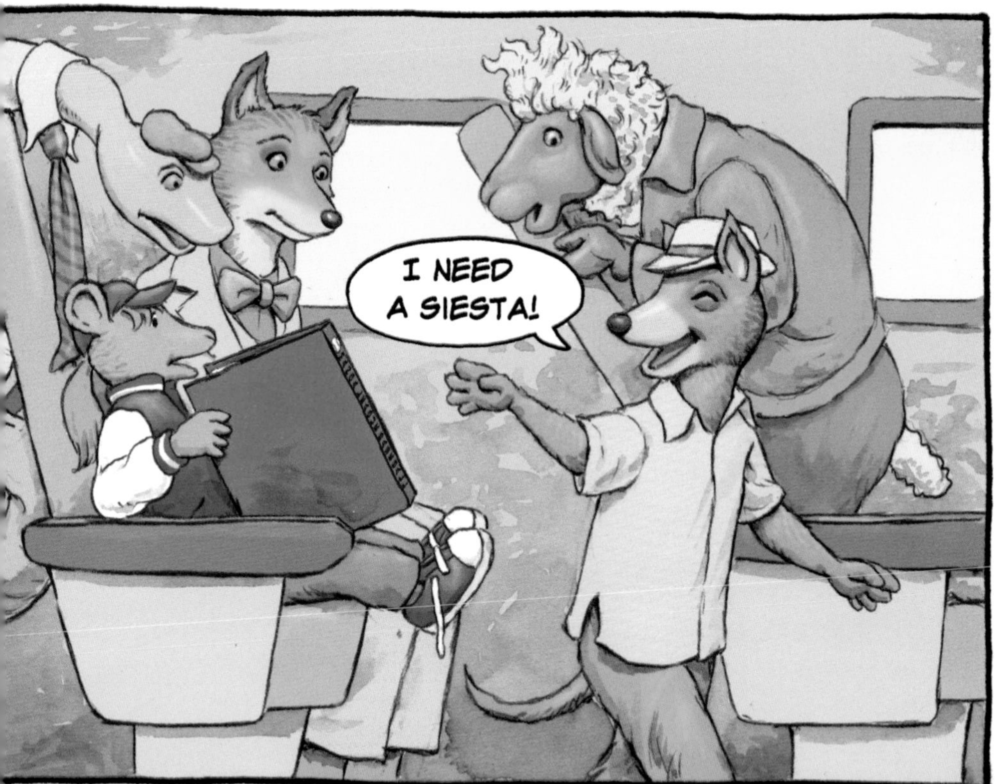
I NEED A SIESTA!

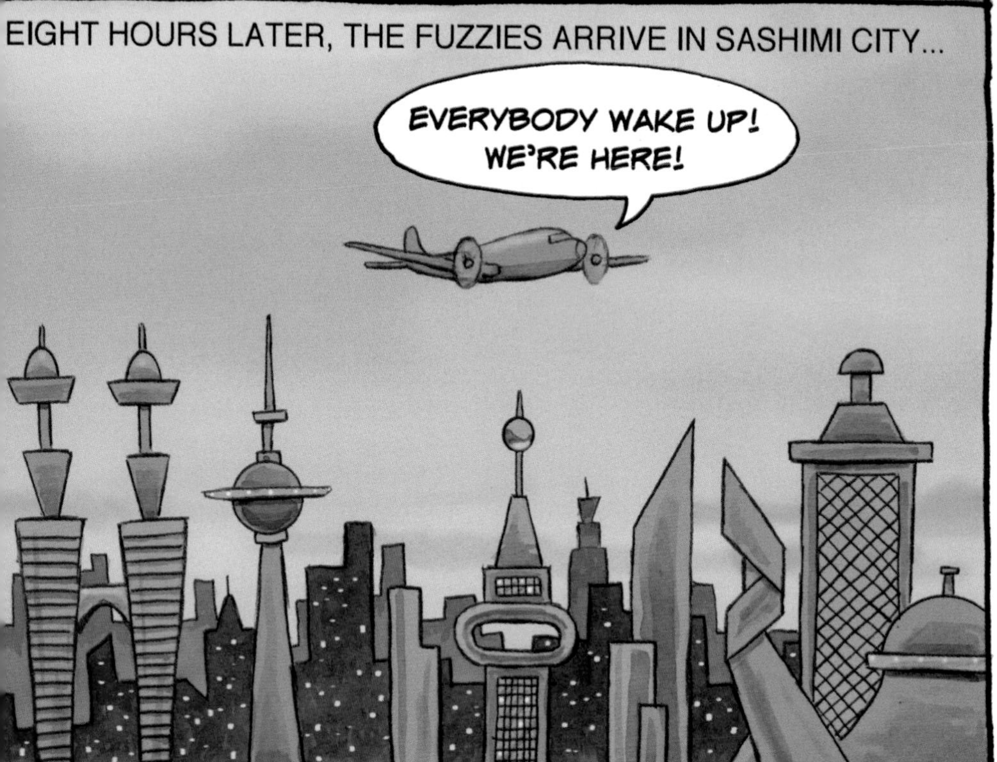
EIGHT HOURS LATER, THE FUZZIES ARRIVE IN SASHIMI CITY...
EVERYBODY WAKE UP! WE'RE HERE!

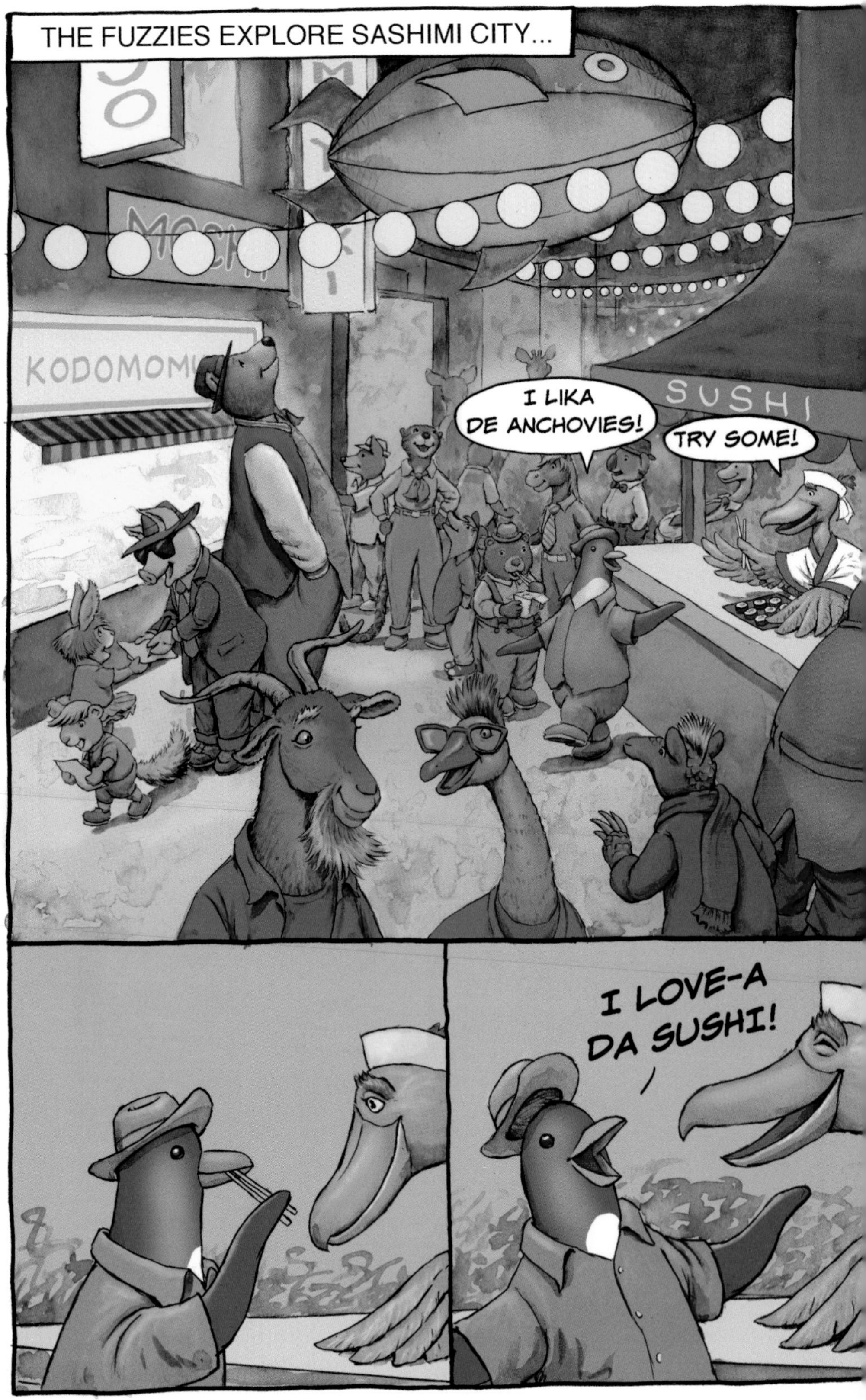
THE FUZZIES EXPLORE SASHIMI CITY...
KODOMOMU
SUSHI
I LIKA DE ANCHOVIES!
TRY SOME!
I LOVE-A DA SUSHI!

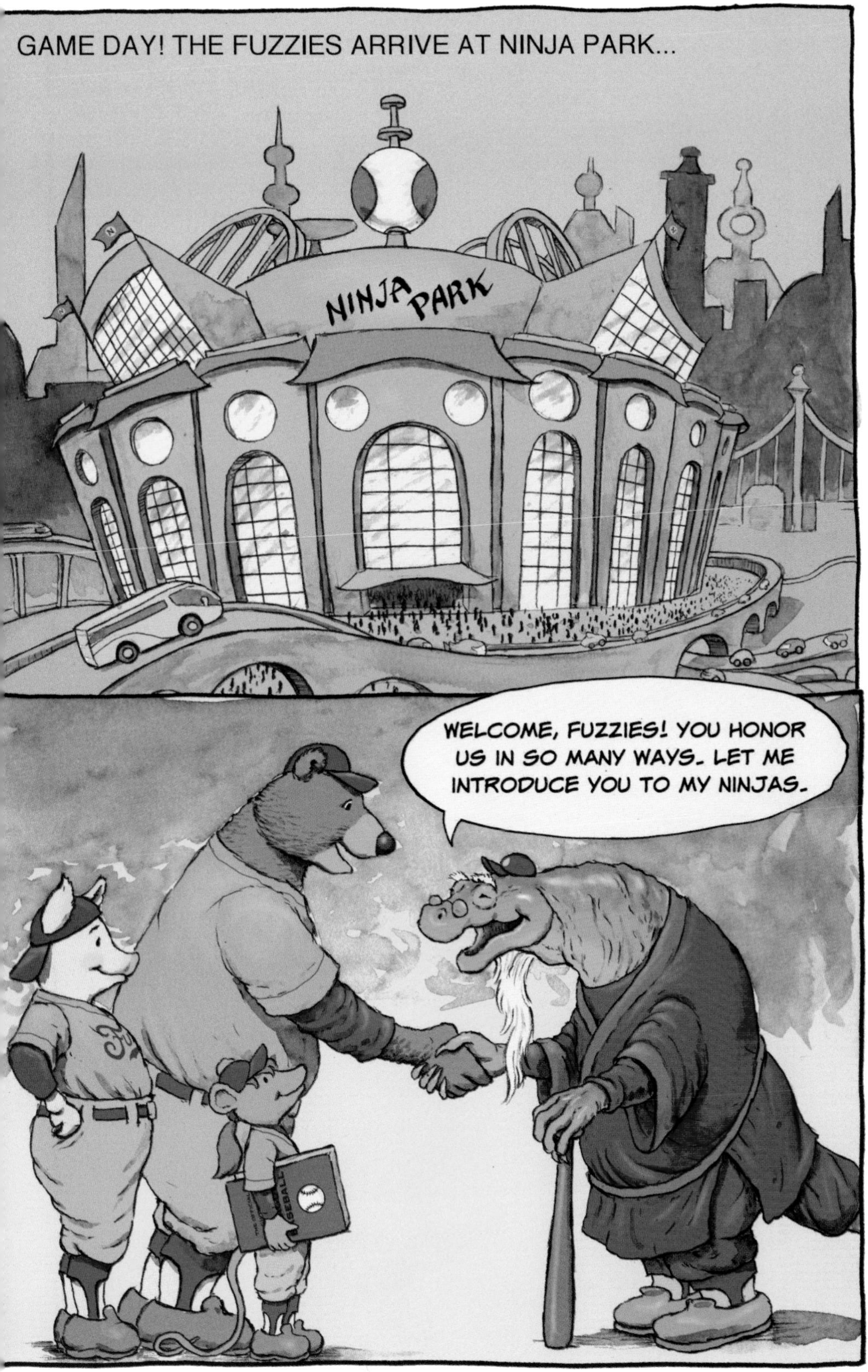
GAME DAY! THE FUZZIES ARRIVE AT NINJA PARK...
NINJA PARK
WELCOME, FUZZIES! YOU HONOR US IN SO MANY WAYS. LET ME INTRODUCE YOU TO MY NINJAS.

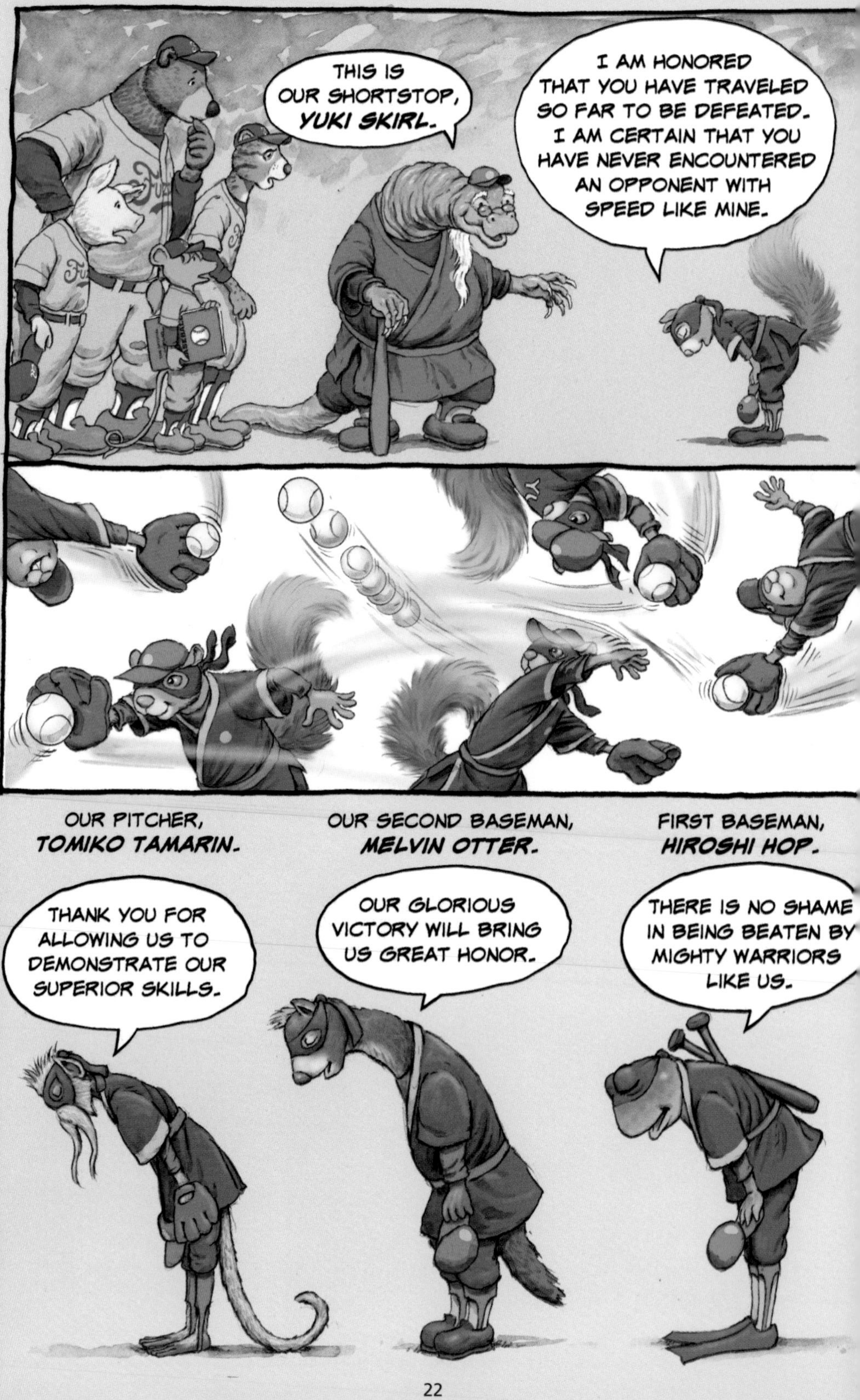
THIS IS OUR SHORTSTOP, YUKI SKIRL.
I AM HONORED THAT YOU HAVE TRAVELED SO FAR TO BE DEFEATED. I AM CERTAIN THAT YOU HAVE NEVER ENCOUNTERED AN OPPONENT WITH SPEED LIKE MINE.
OUR PITCHER, TOMIKO TAMARIN.
THANK YOU FOR ALLOWING US TO DEMONSTRATE OUR SUPERIOR SKILLS.
OUR SECOND BASEMAN, MELVIN OTTER.
OUR GLORIOUS VICTORY WILL BRING US GREAT HONOR.
FIRST BASEMAN, HIROSHI HOP.
THERE IS NO SHAME IN BEING BEATEN BY MIGHTY WARRIORS LIKE US.

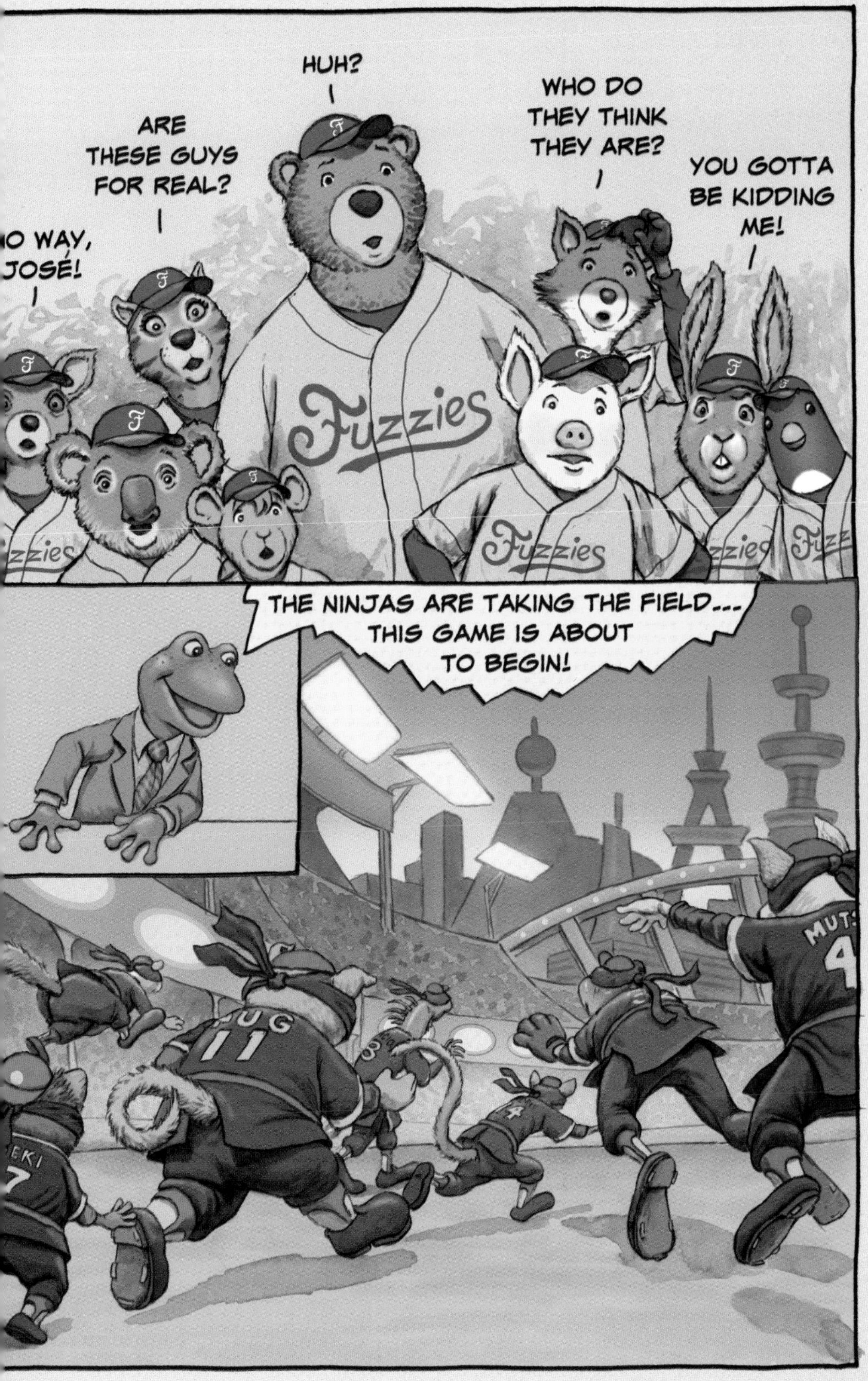
O WAY, JOSÉ!
ARE THESE GUYS FOR REAL?
HUH?
WHO DO THEY THINK THEY ARE?
YOU GOTTA BE KIDDING ME!
Fuzzies
THE NINJAS ARE TAKING THE FIELD... THIS GAME IS ABOUT TO BEGIN!

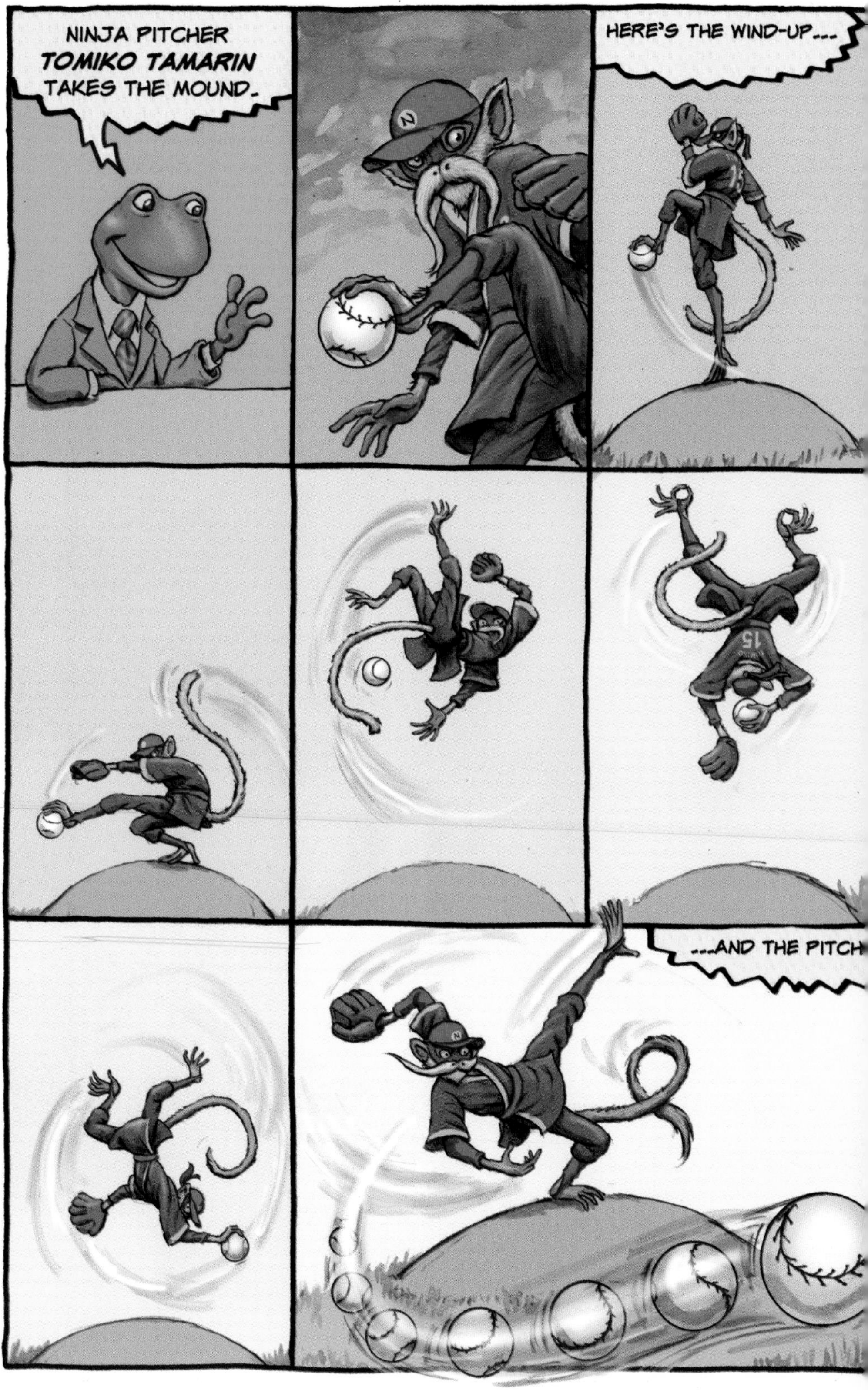
NINJA PITCHER
TOMIKO TAMARIN
TAKES THE MOUND...
HERE'S THE WIND-UP...
...AND THE PITCH

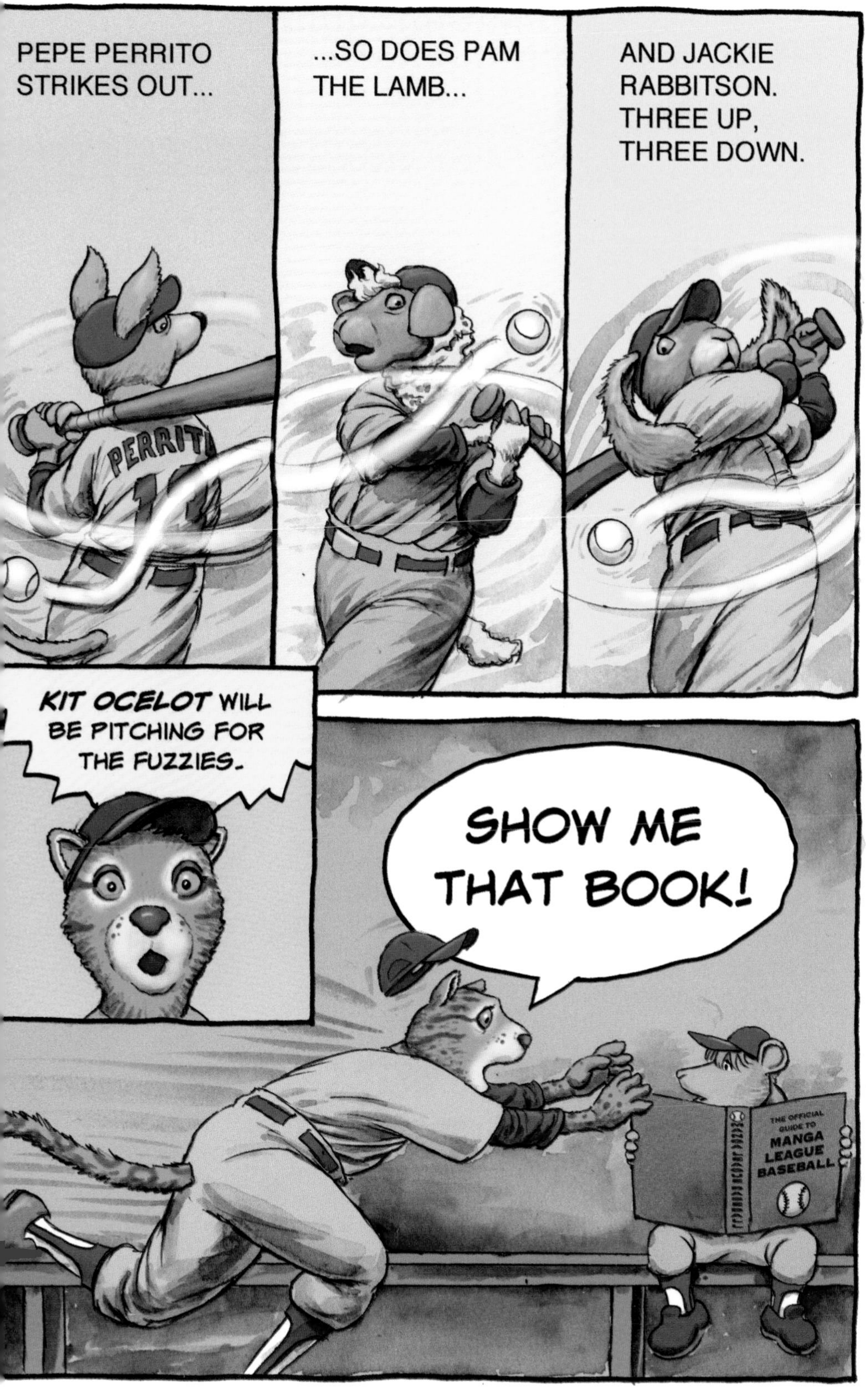
PEPE PERRITO STRIKES OUT...
PERRITO 14
...SO DOES PAM THE LAMB...
AND JACKIE RABBITSON. THREE UP, THREE DOWN.
KIT OCELOT WILL BE PITCHING FOR THE FUZZIES.
SHOW ME THAT BOOK!
THE OFFICIAL GUIDE TO MANGA LEAGUE BASEBALL

THERE ARE MANY DIFFERENT TYPES OF PITCHES IN MANGA BASEBALL.

THE CRISS-CROSS TURTLE

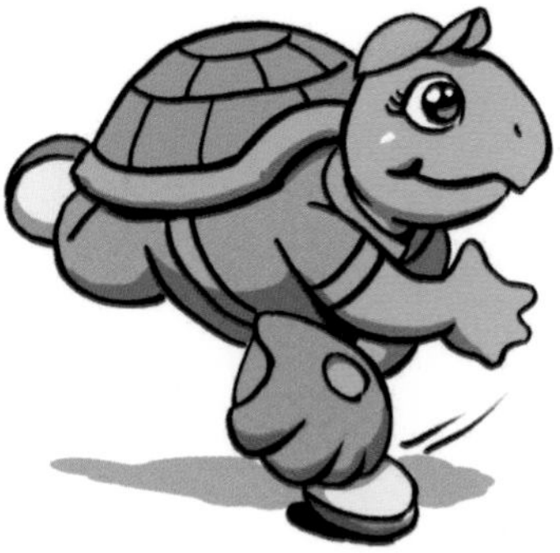

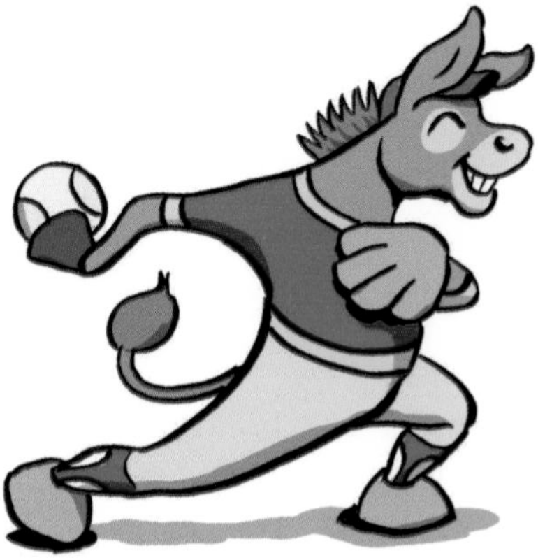

THE BOWLING DONKEY

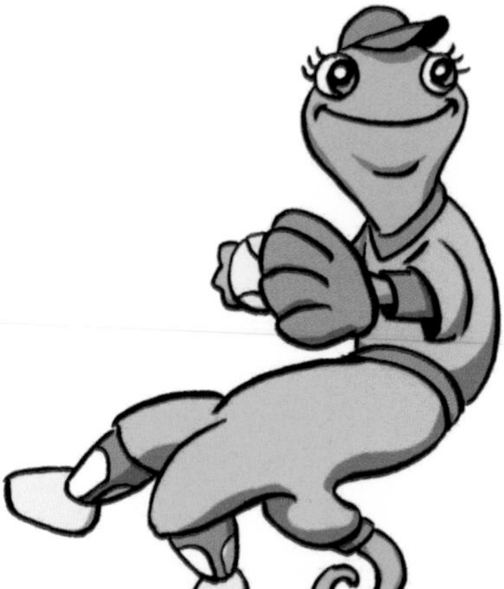

THE SPRINGY SALAMANDER

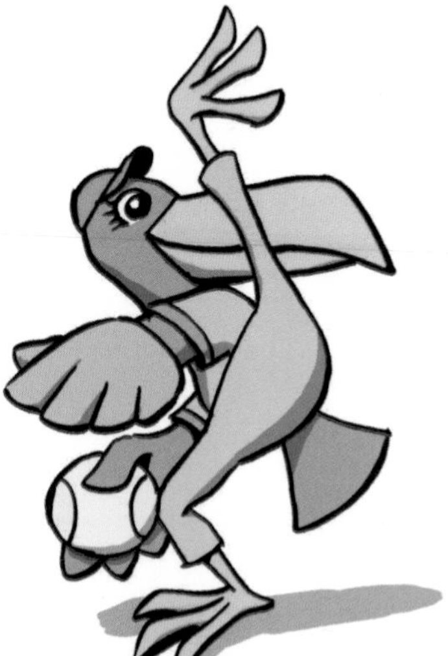

THE HIGH STEP TOUCAN

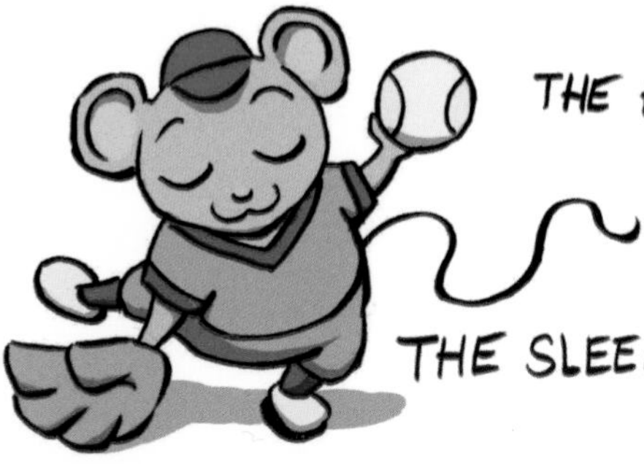

THE SLEEPY MOUSE

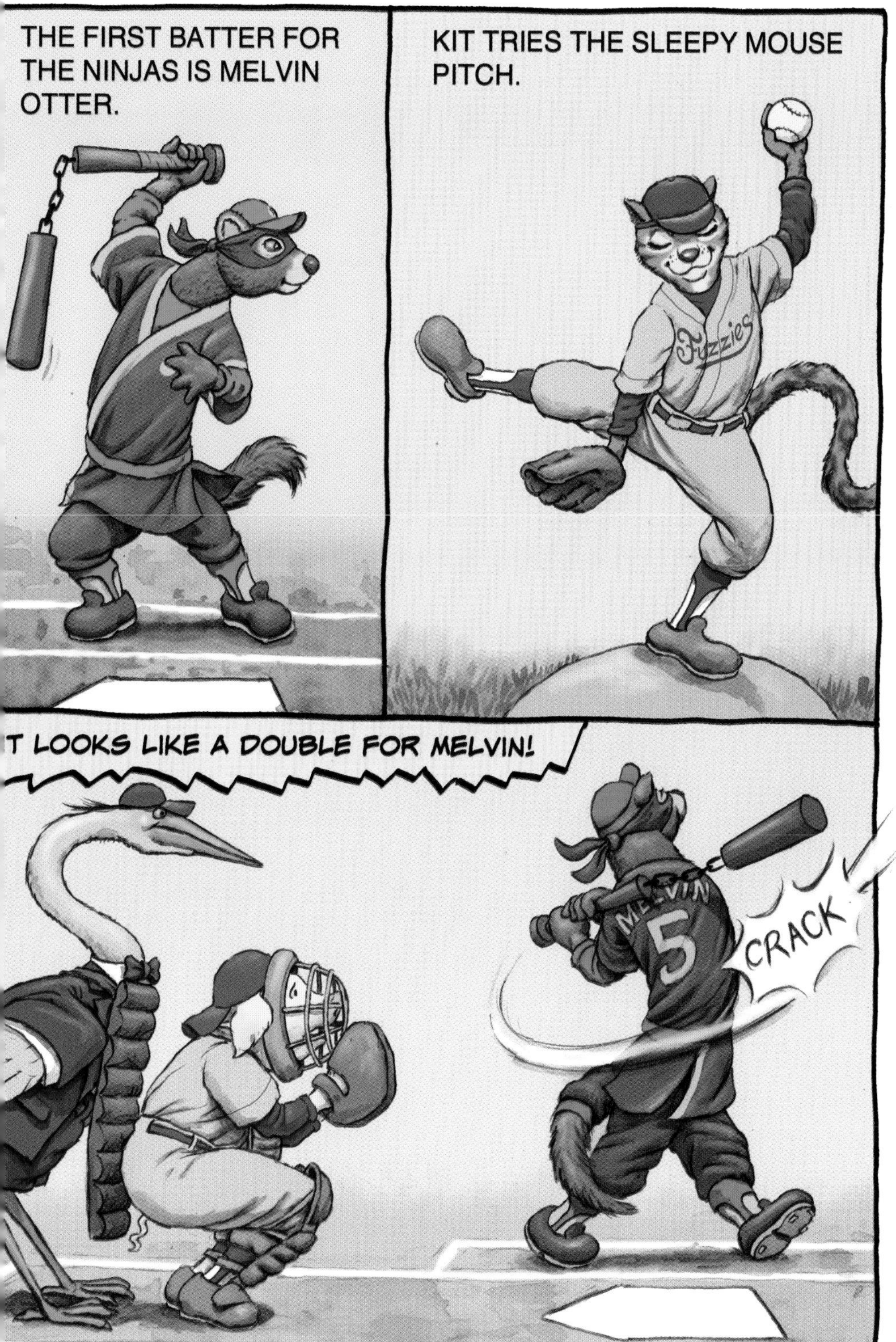
THE FIRST BATTER FOR THE NINJAS IS MELVIN OTTER.
KIT TRIES THE SLEEPY MOUSE PITCH.
Fuzzies
T LOOKS LIKE A DOUBLE FOR MELVIN!
MELVIN
5
CRACK

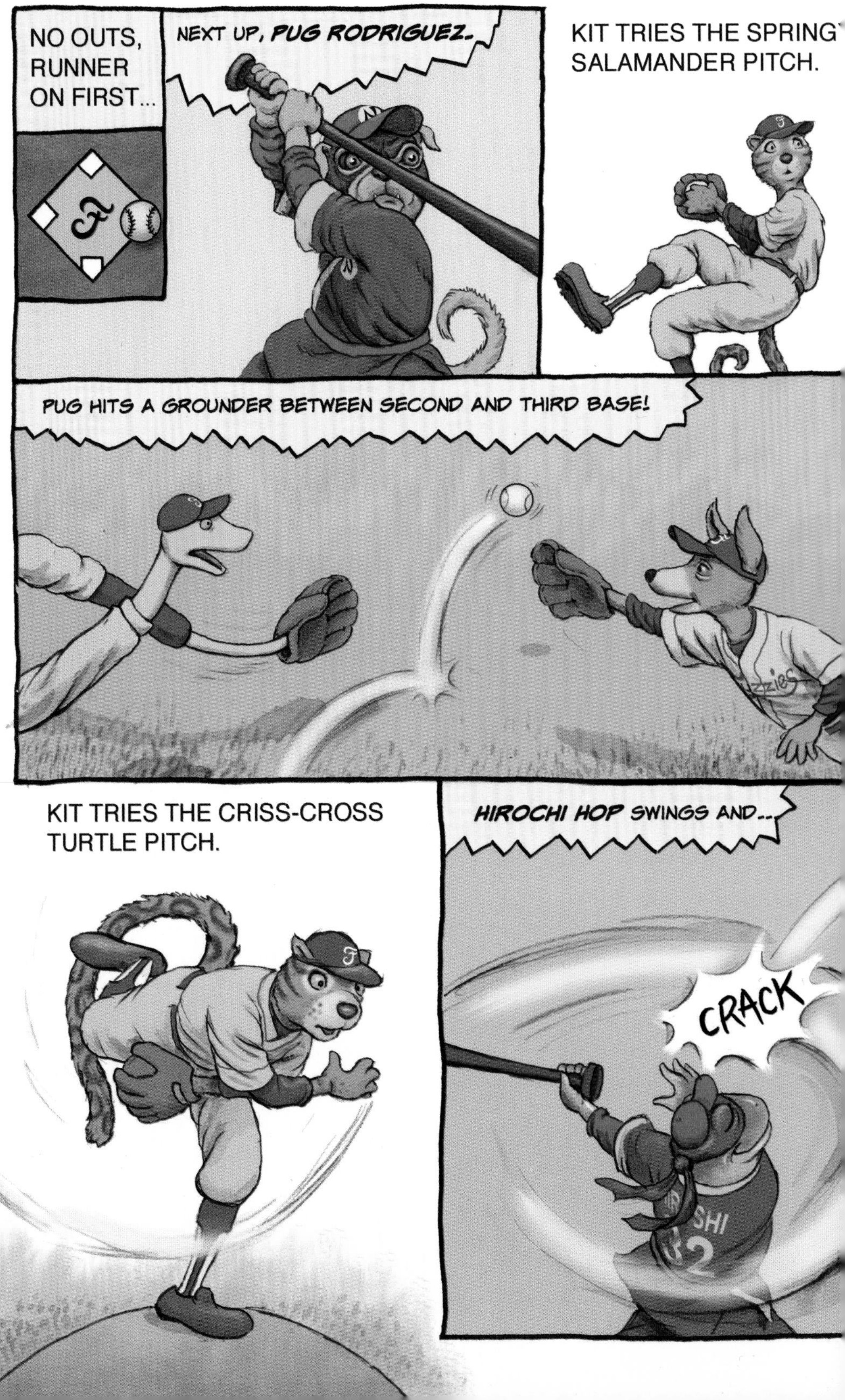
NO OUTS, RUNNER ON FIRST...
NEXT UP, PUG RODRIGUEZ.
KIT TRIES THE SPRING SALAMANDER PITCH.
PUG HITS A GROUNDER BETWEEN SECOND AND THIRD BASE!
KIT TRIES THE CRISS-CROSS TURTLE PITCH.
HIROCHI HOP SWINGS AND...
CRACK

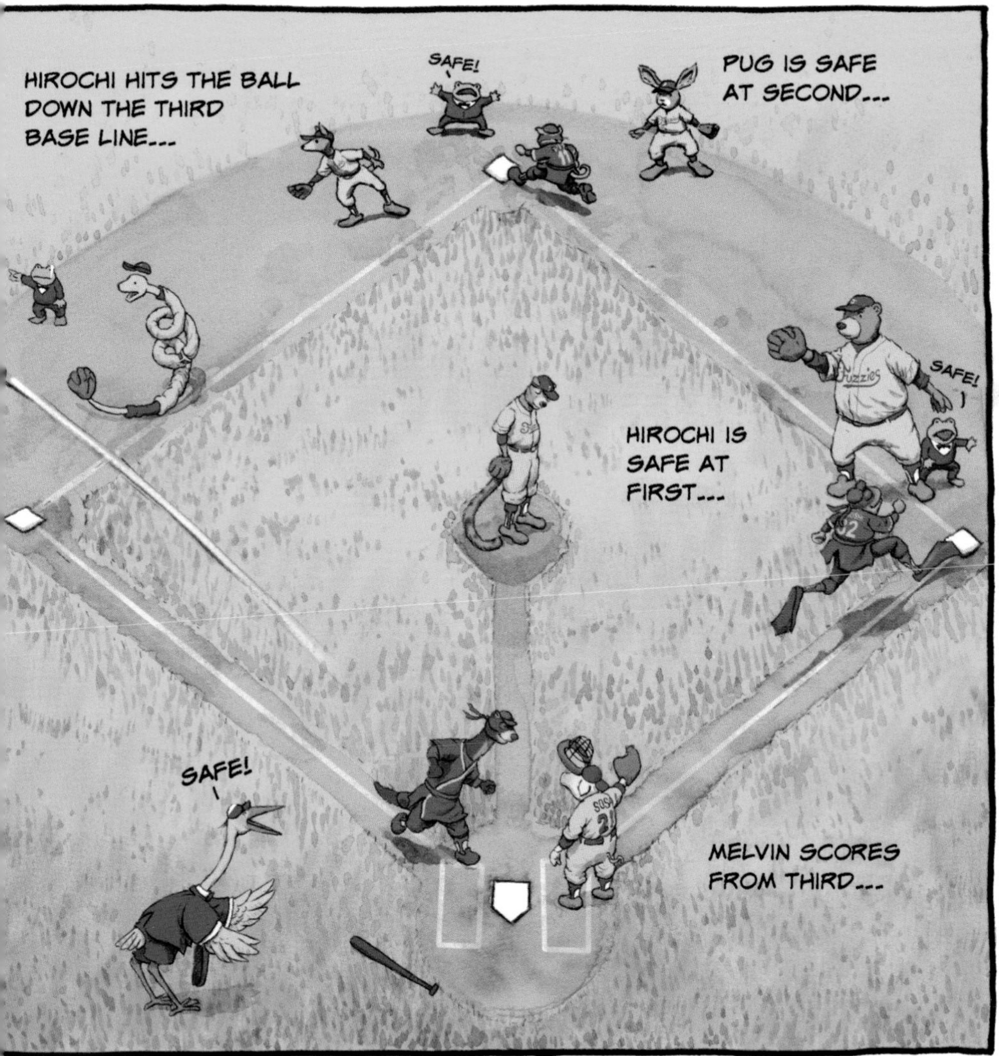
HIROCHI HITS THE BALL DOWN THE THIRD BASE LINE...
SAFE!
PUG IS SAFE AT SECOND...
SAFE!
HIROCHI IS SAFE AT FIRST...
SAFE!
MELVIN SCORES FROM THIRD...

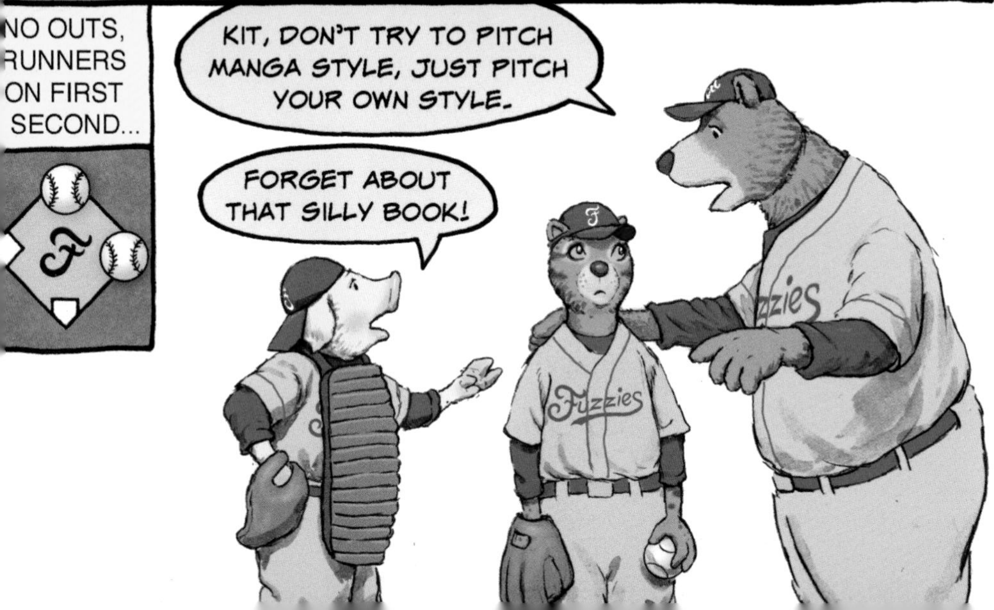
NO OUTS, RUNNERS ON FIRST SECOND...
KIT, DON'T TRY TO PITCH MANGA STYLE, JUST PITCH YOUR OWN STYLE.
FORGET ABOUT THAT SILLY BOOK!

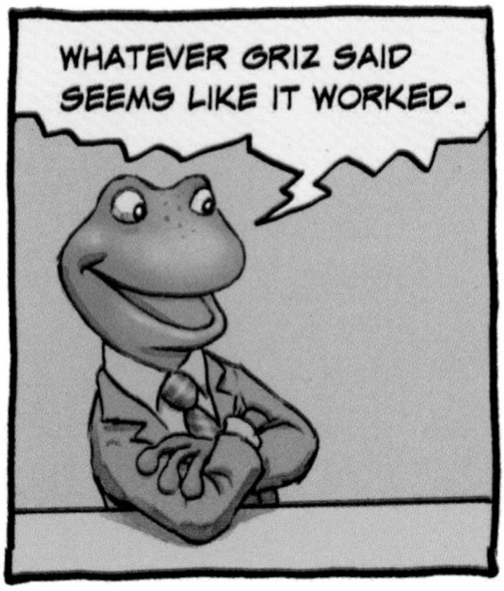
WHATEVER GRIZ SAID SEEMS LIKE IT WORKED.

KIT STOPS THINKING ABOUT PITCHING MANGA STYLE. SHE FOCUSES ON PITCHING HER OWN STYLE...

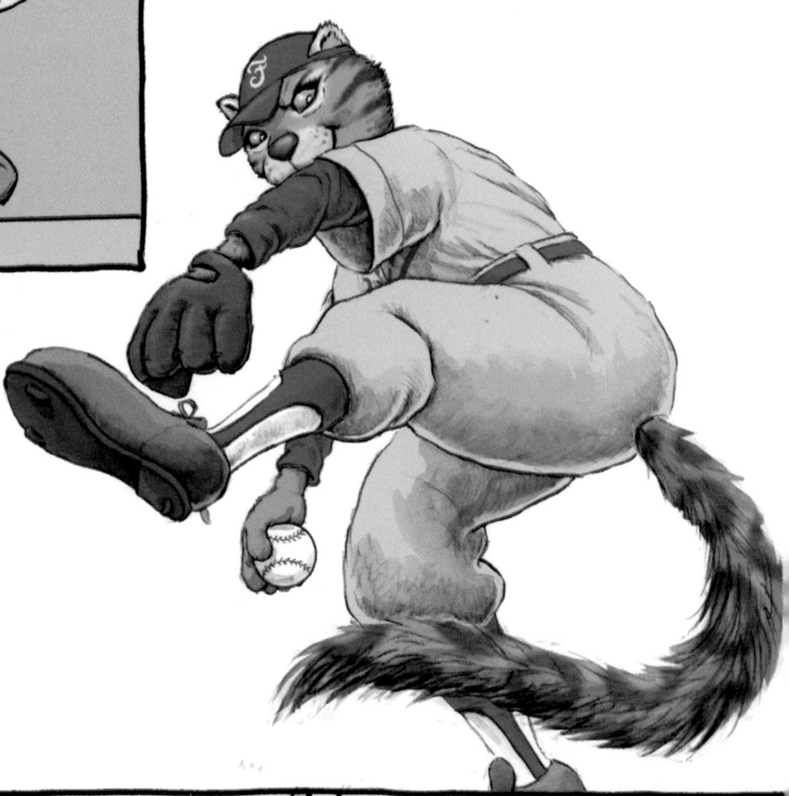

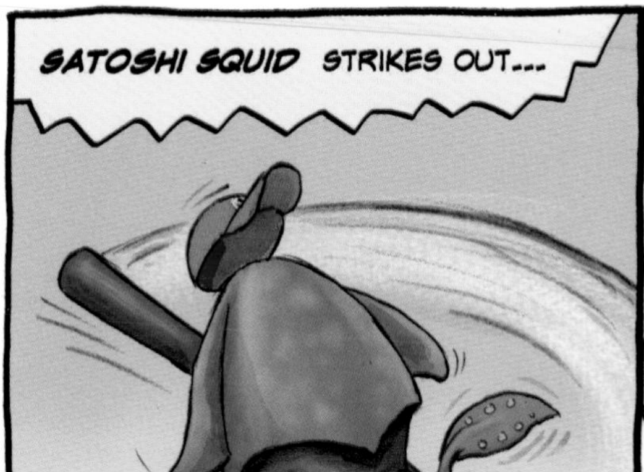
SATOSHI SQUID STRIKES OUT...

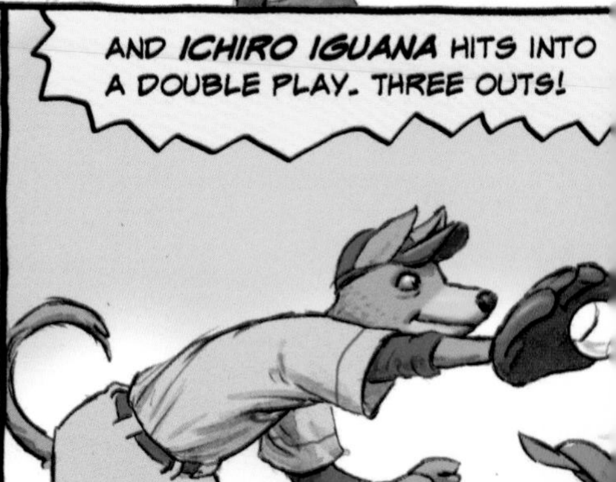
AND ICHIRO IGUANA HITS INTO A DOUBLE PLAY. THREE OUTS!

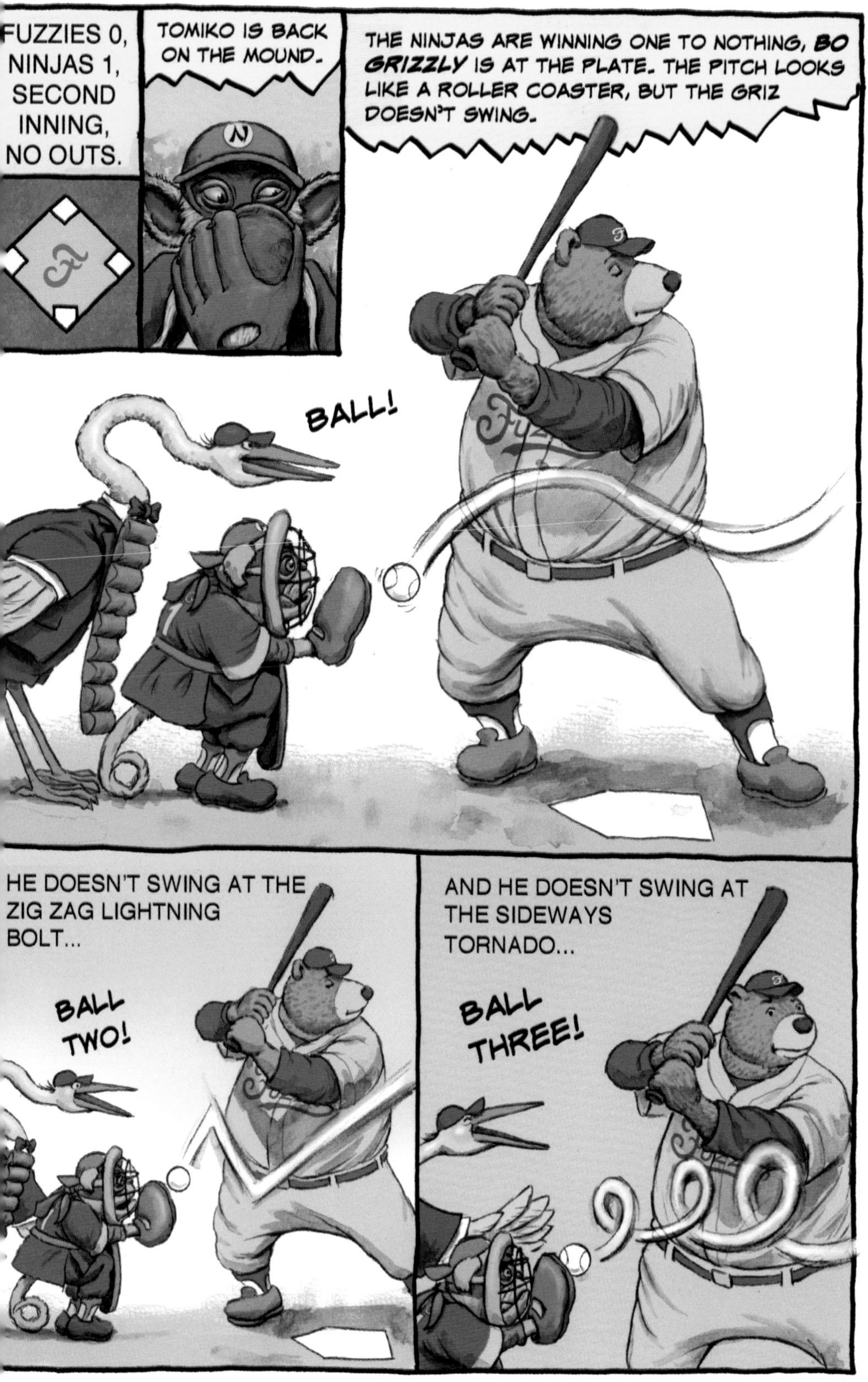

FUZZIES 0, NINJAS 1, SECOND INNING, NO OUTS.
TOMIKO IS BACK ON THE MOUND.
THE NINJAS ARE WINNING ONE TO NOTHING, BO GRIZZLY IS AT THE PLATE. THE PITCH LOOKS LIKE A ROLLER COASTER, BUT THE GRIZ DOESN'T SWING.
BALL!
HE DOESN'T SWING AT THE ZIG ZAG LIGHTNING BOLT...
BALL TWO!
AND HE DOESN'T SWING AT THE SIDEWAYS TORNADO...
BALL THREE!

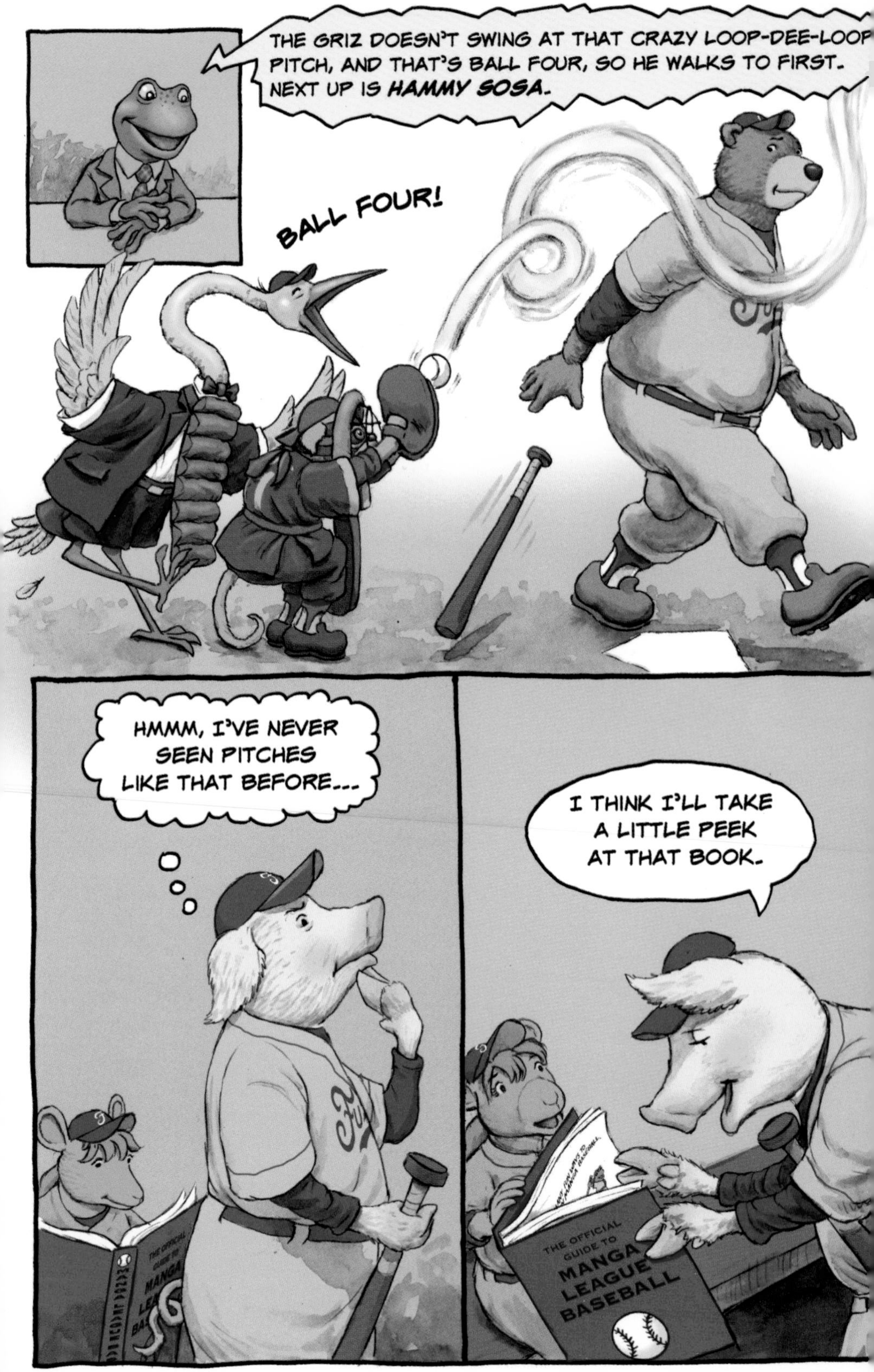
THE GRIZ DOESN'T SWING AT THAT CRAZY LOOP-DEE-LOOP PITCH, AND THAT'S BALL FOUR, SO HE WALKS TO FIRST. NEXT UP IS ***HAMMY SOSA.***
BALL FOUR!
HMMM, I'VE NEVER SEEN PITCHES LIKE THAT BEFORE...
I THINK I'LL TAKE A LITTLE PEEK AT THAT BOOK.
THE OFFICIAL GUIDE TO MANGA LEAGUE BASEBALL

THERE ARE MANY FUN WAYS TO HOLD THE BAT IN MANGA BASEBALL.

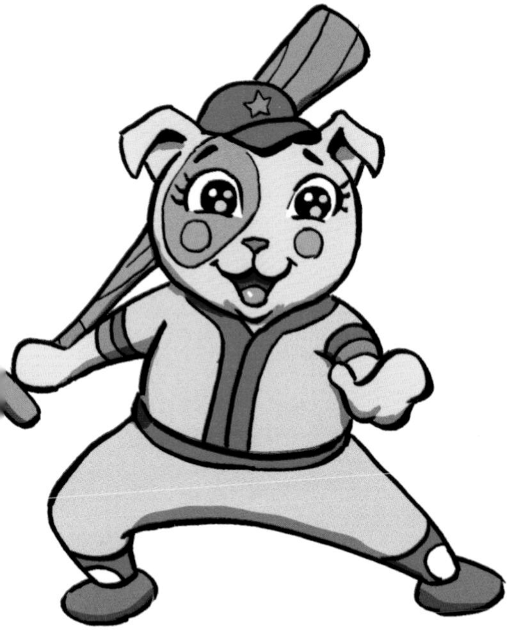

JAZZY SWING

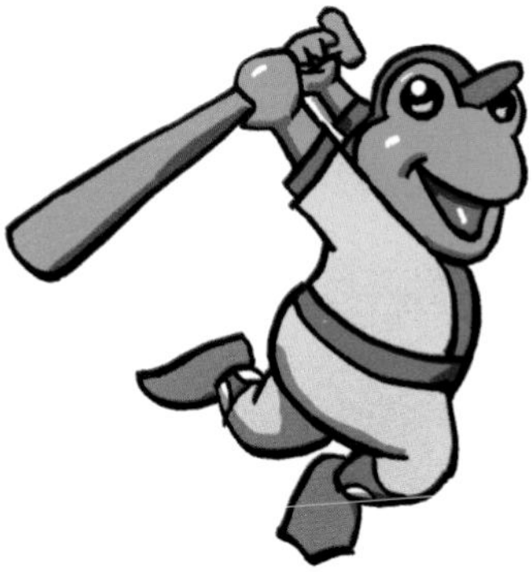

CHOP-CHOP SWING

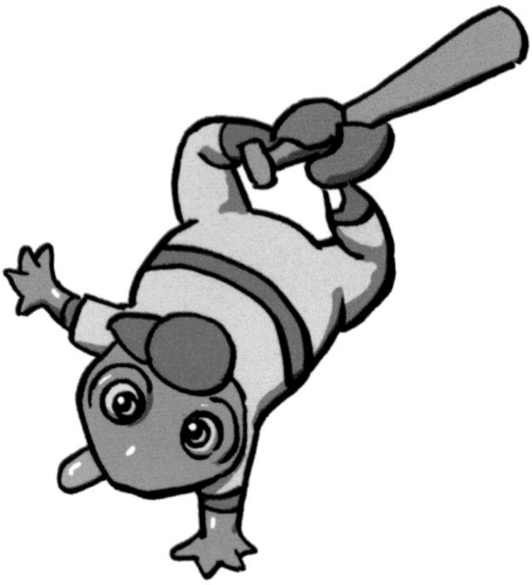

BUTTS UP SWING

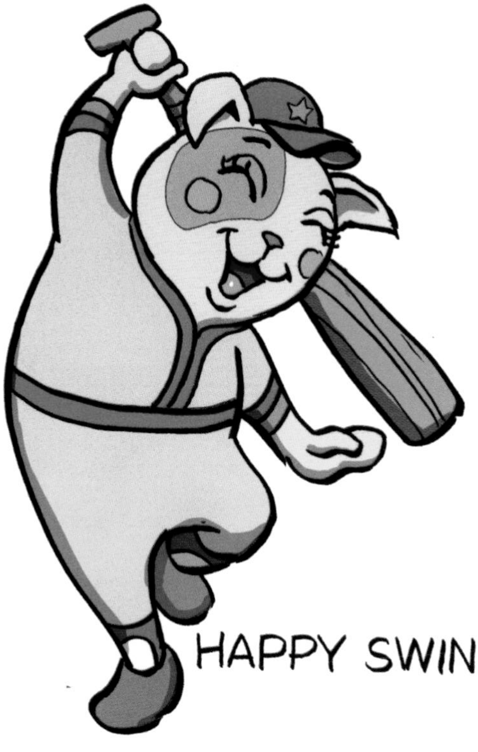

HAPPY SWING

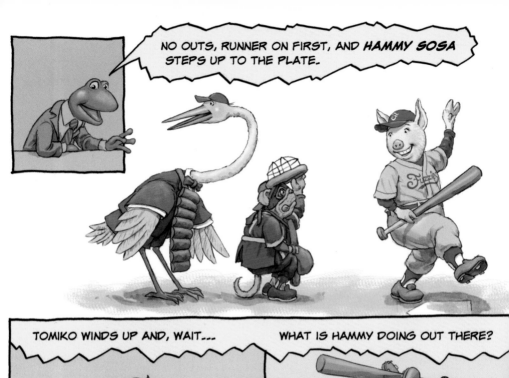

NO OUTS, RUNNER ON FIRST, AND *HAMMY SOSA* STEPS UP TO THE PLATE.

TOMIKO WINDS UP AND, WAIT.... WHAT IS HAMMY DOING OUT THERE?

HERE'S THE PITCH....

STRIKE ONE!

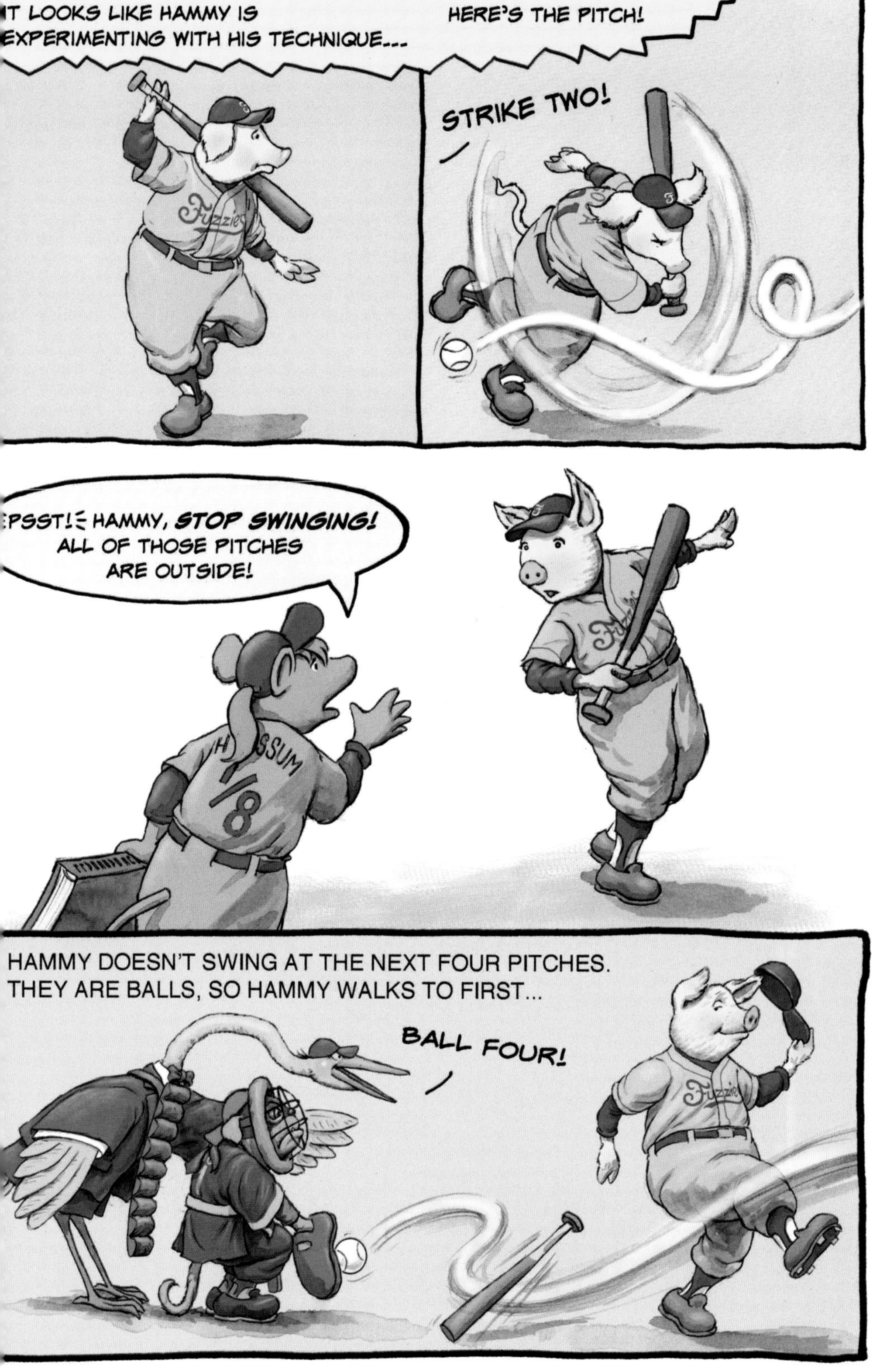
IT LOOKS LIKE HAMMY IS EXPERIMENTING WITH HIS TECHNIQUE...
HERE'S THE PITCH!
STRIKE TWO!
PSST! HAMMY, ***STOP SWINGING!*** ALL OF THOSE PITCHES ARE OUTSIDE!
HAMMY DOESN'T SWING AT THE NEXT FOUR PITCHES. THEY ARE BALLS, SO HAMMY WALKS TO FIRST...
BALL FOUR!

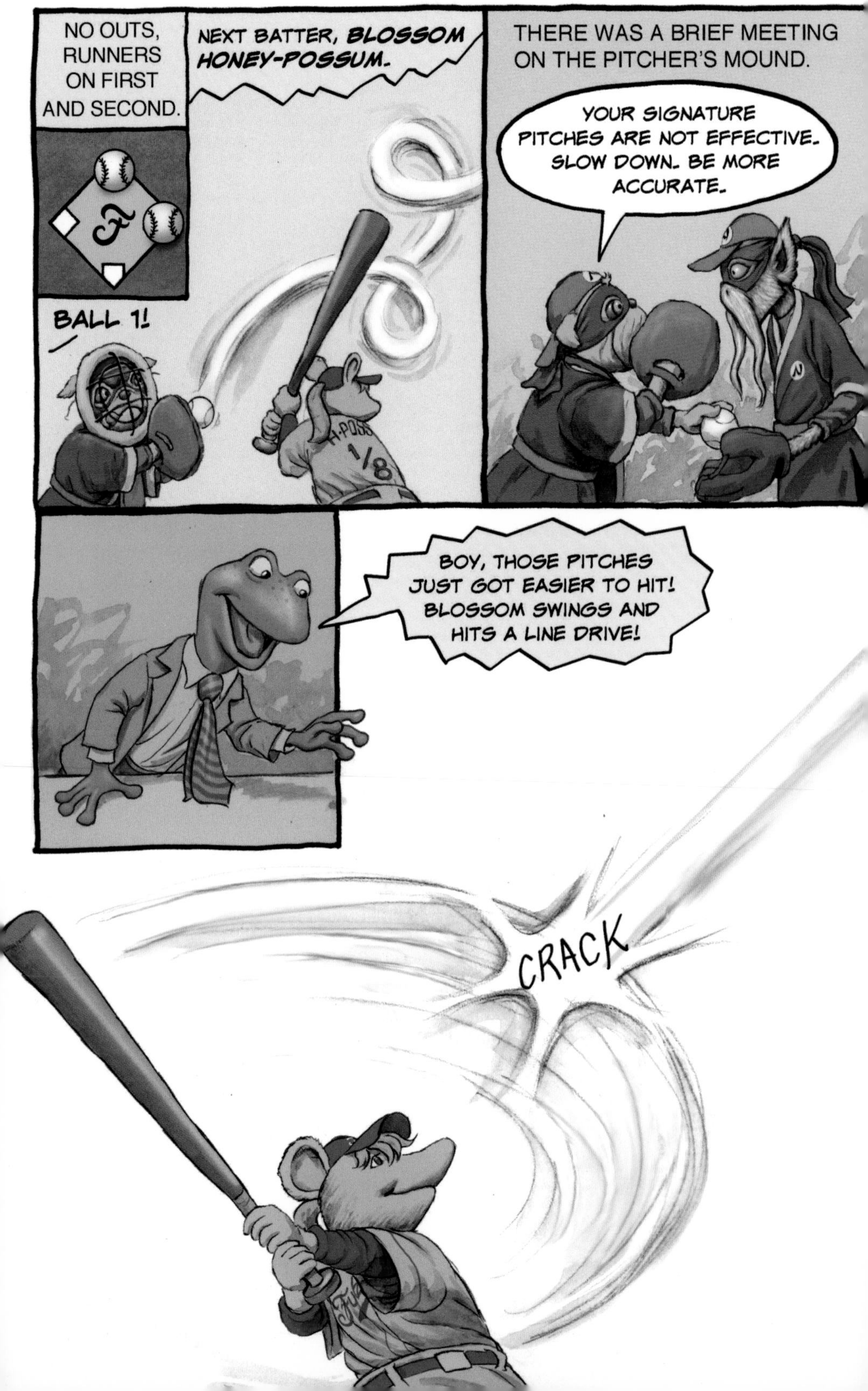
NO OUTS, RUNNERS ON FIRST AND SECOND.
NEXT BATTER, BLOSSOM HONEY-POSSUM.
BALL 1!
THERE WAS A BRIEF MEETING ON THE PITCHER'S MOUND.
YOUR SIGNATURE PITCHES ARE NOT EFFECTIVE. SLOW DOWN. BE MORE ACCURATE.
BOY, THOSE PITCHES JUST GOT EASIER TO HIT! BLOSSOM SWINGS AND HITS A LINE DRIVE!
CRACK

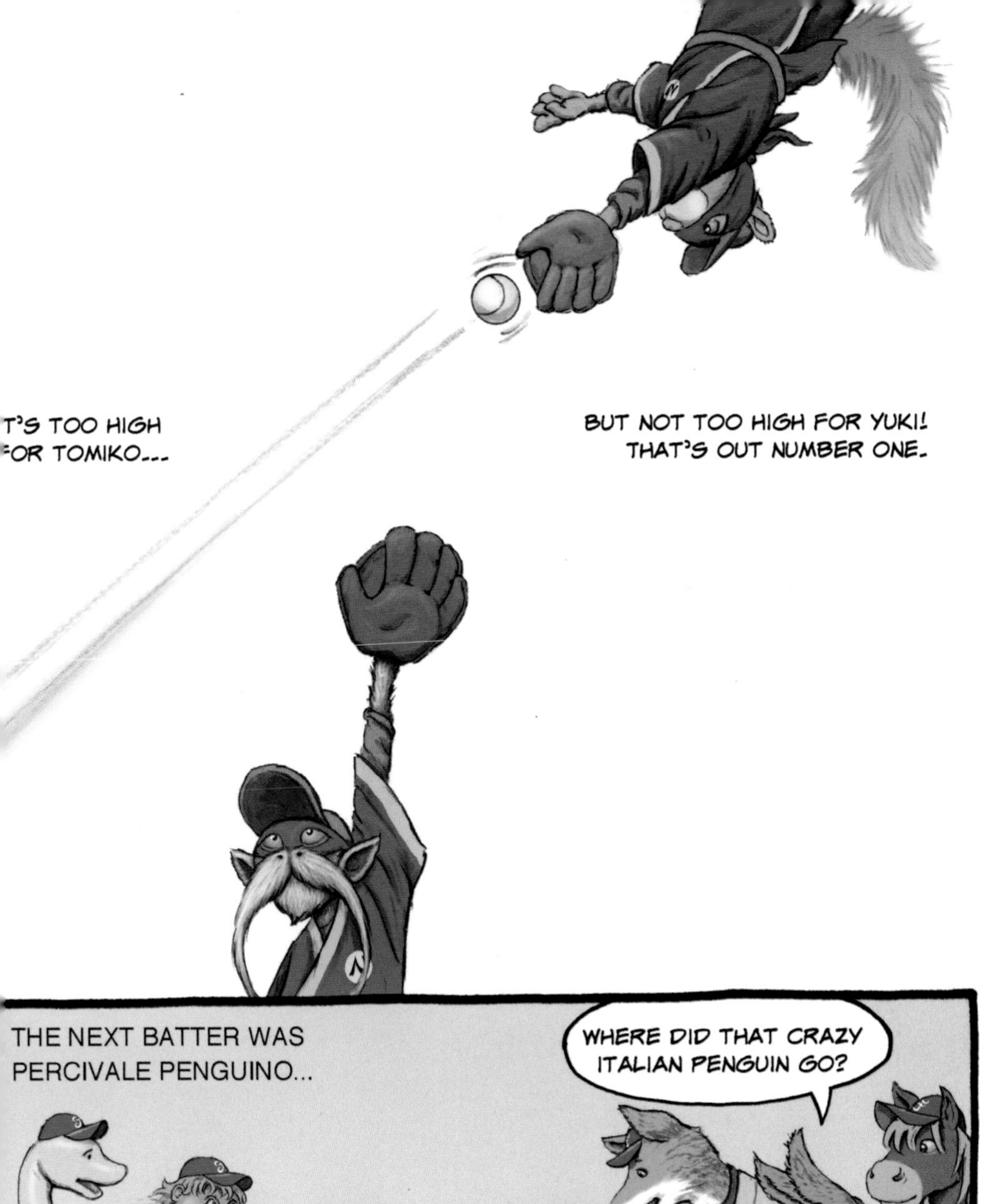

T'S TOO HIGH
FOR TOMIKO...
BUT NOT TOO HIGH FOR YUKI! THAT'S OUT NUMBER ONE.

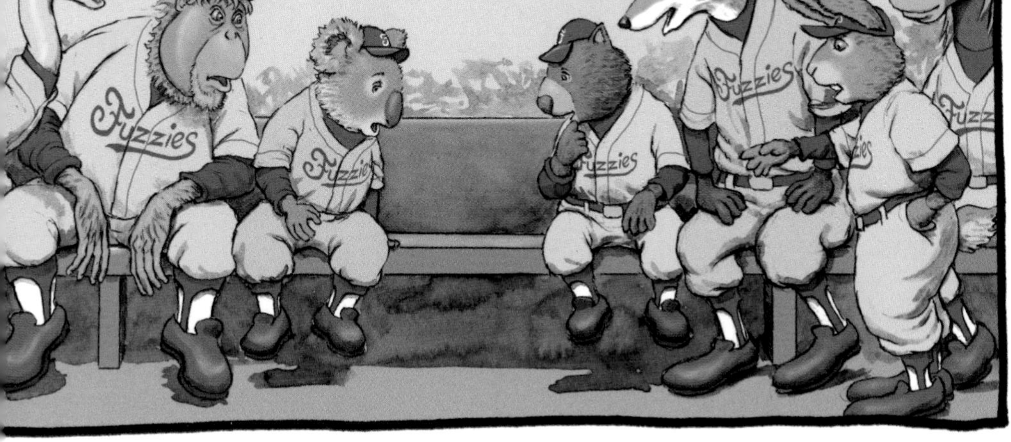

THE NEXT BATTER WAS PERCIVALE PENGUINO...
WHERE DID THAT CRAZY ITALIAN PENGUIN GO?
Fuzzies

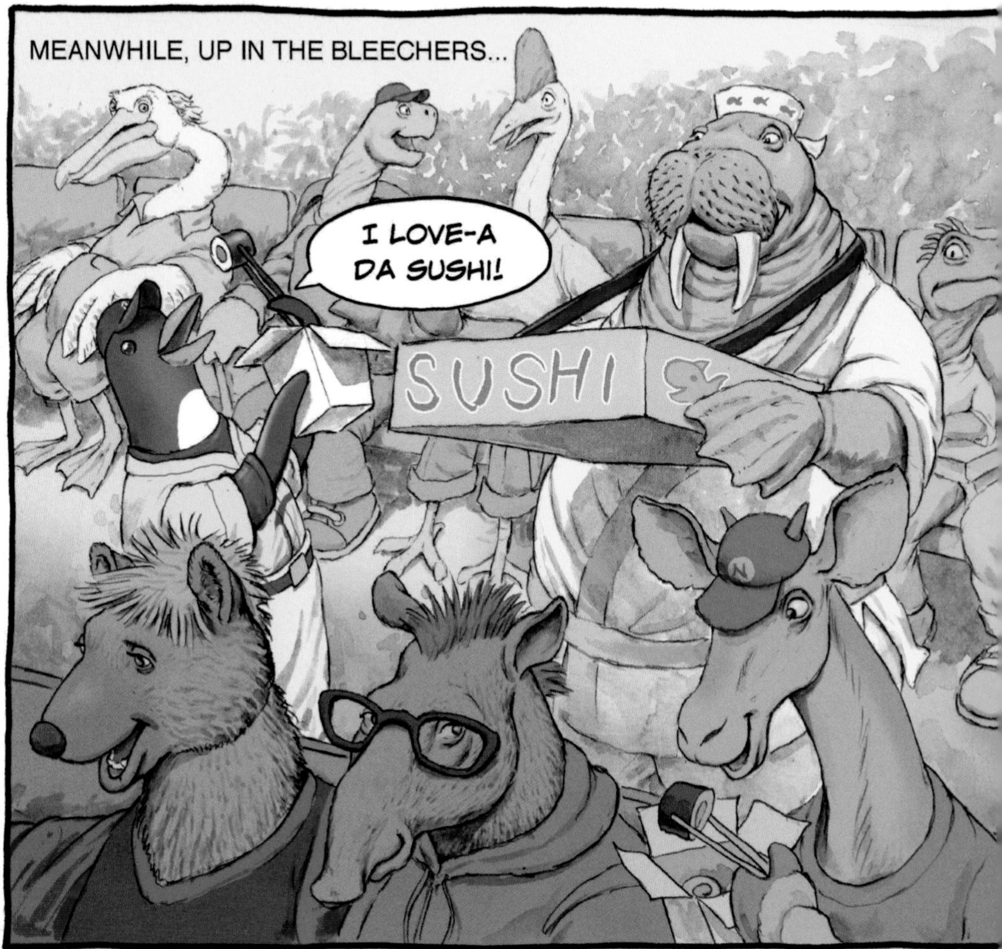
MEANWHILE, UP IN THE BLEECHERS...
I LOVE-A DA SUSHI!
SUSHI

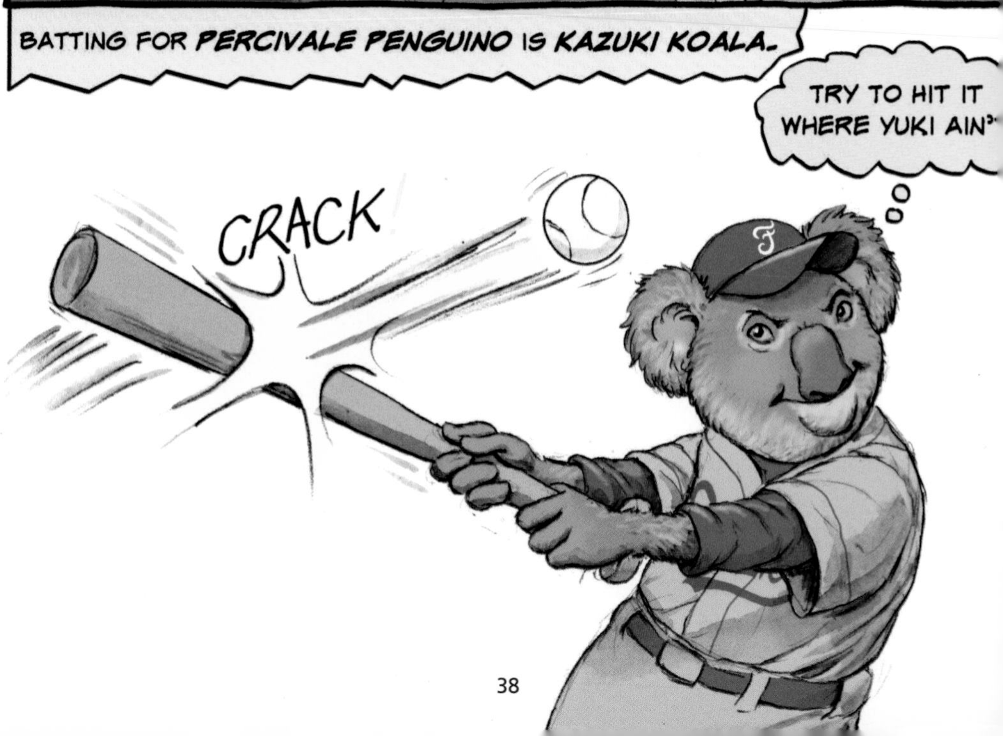
BATTING FOR *PERCIVALE PENGUINO* IS *KAZUKI KOALA*.
TRY TO HIT IT WHERE YUKI AIN'
CRACK

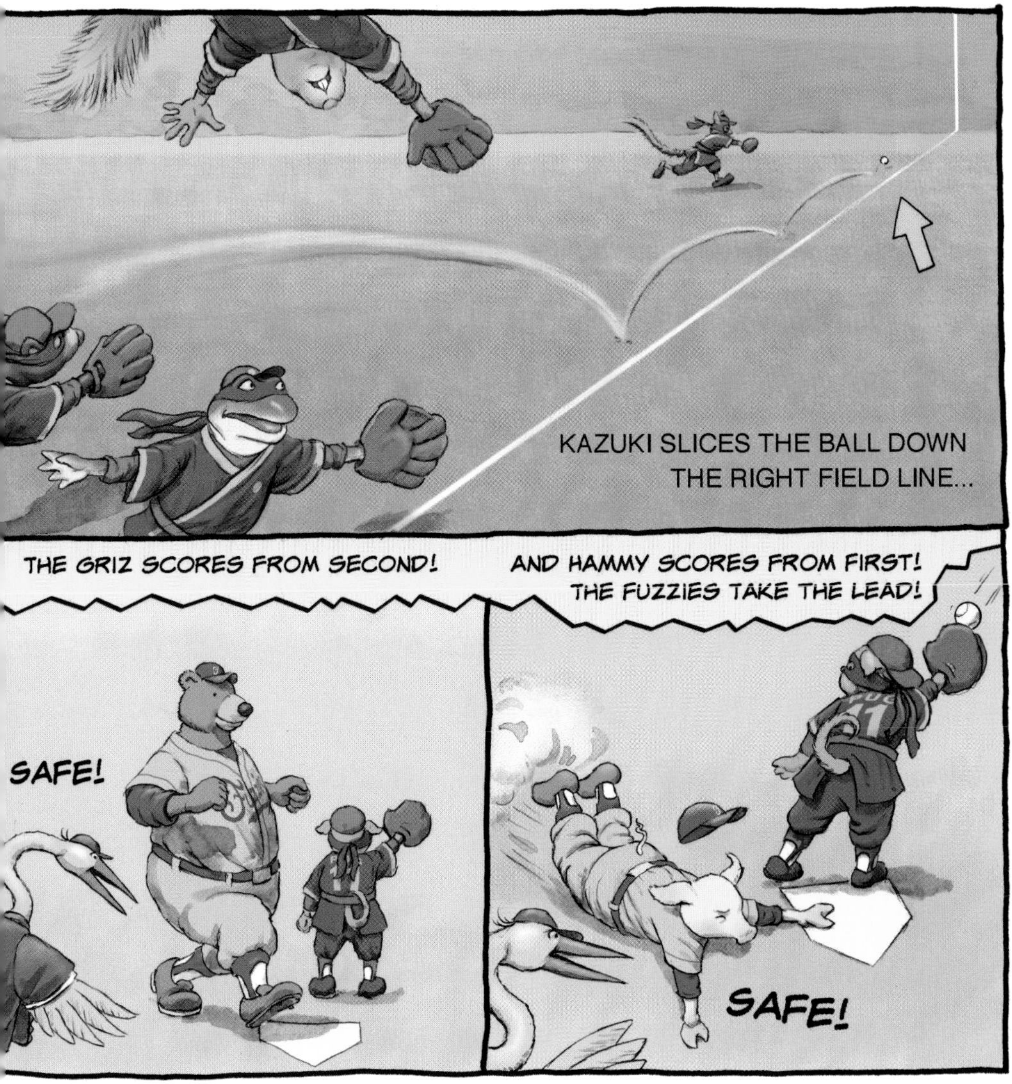
KAZUKI SLICES THE BALL DOWN
THE RIGHT FIELD LINE...
THE GRIZ SCORES FROM SECOND!
SAFE!
AND HAMMY SCORES FROM FIRST!
THE FUZZIES TAKE THE LEAD!
SAFE!

ZUKI IS SAFE AT THIRD. NEXT UP: LARRY BOA...

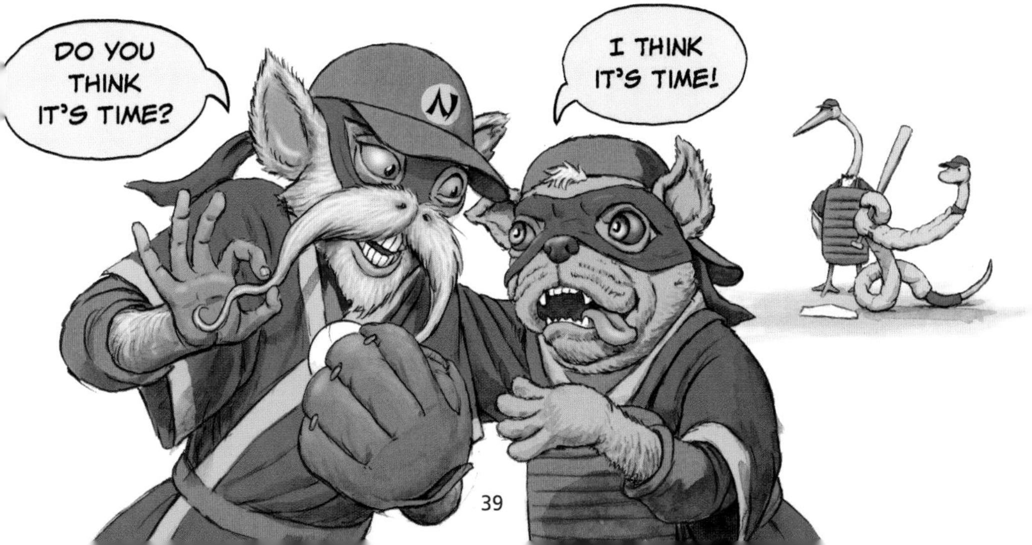
DO YOU
THINK
IT'S TIME?
I THINK
IT'S TIME!

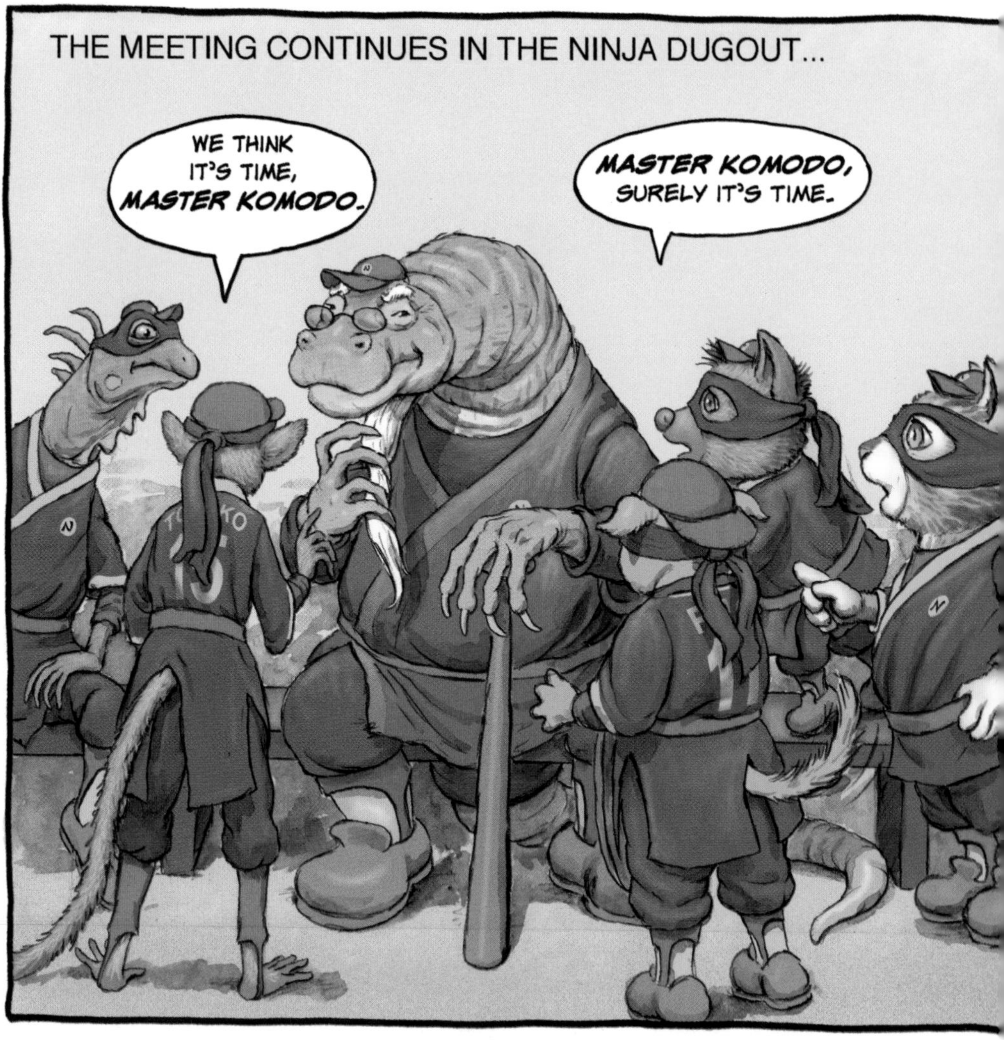
THE MEETING CONTINUES IN THE NINJA DUGOUT...
WE THINK IT'S TIME, MASTER KOMODO.
MASTER KOMODO, SURELY IT'S TIME.

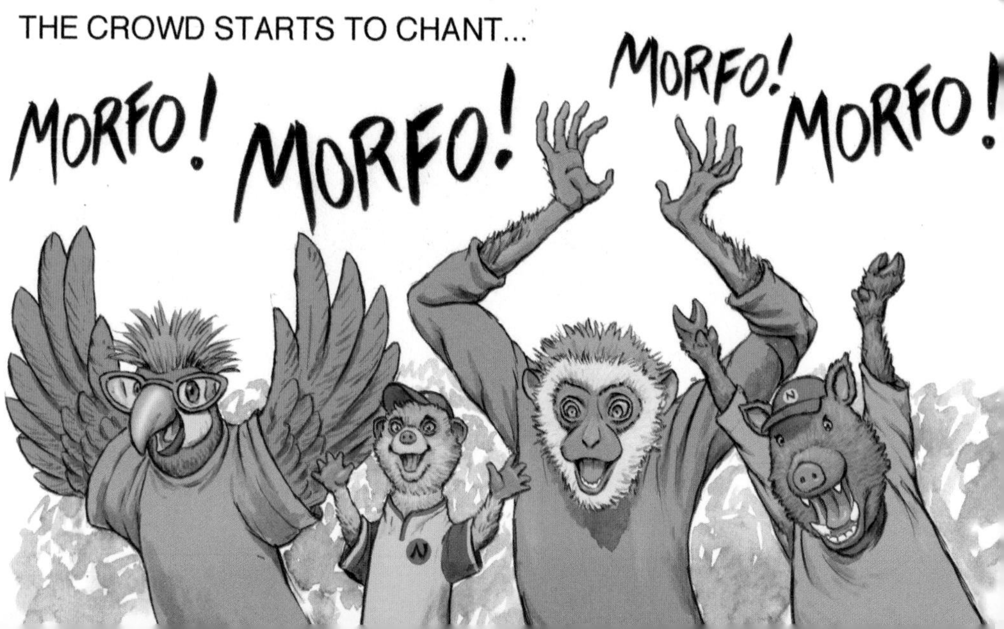
THE CROWD STARTS TO CHANT...
MORFO!
MORFO!
MORFO!
MORFO!

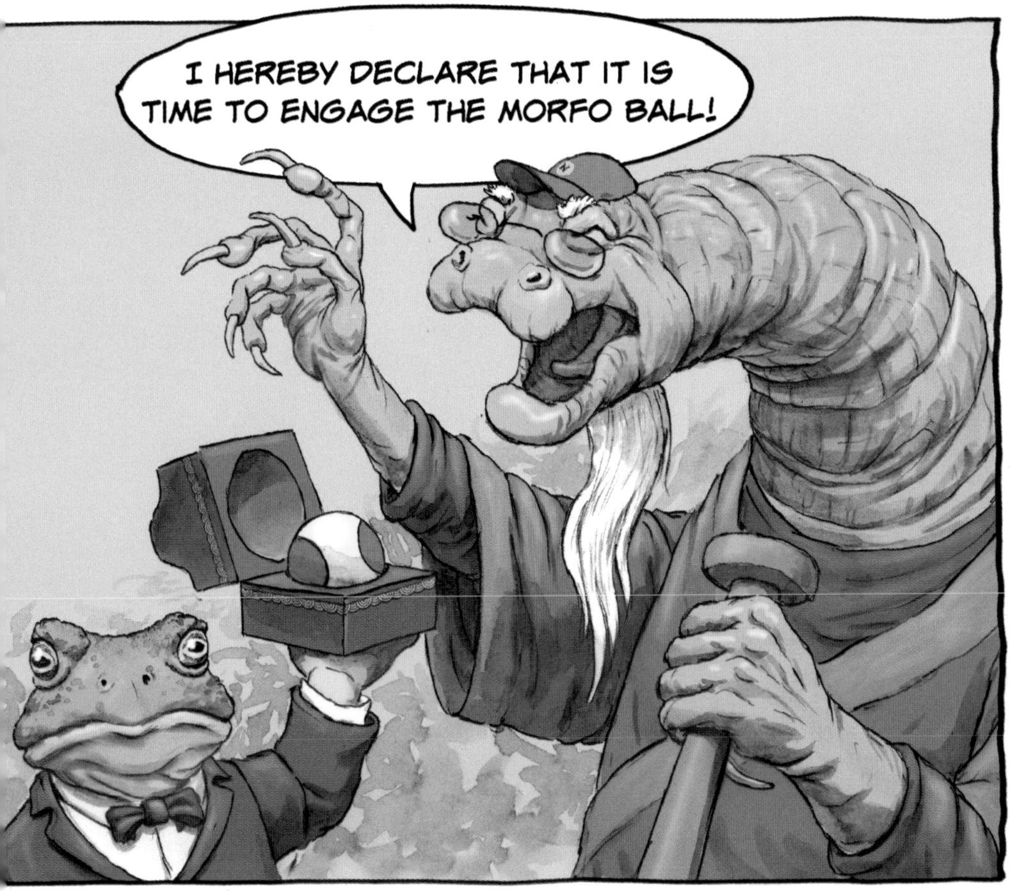
I HEREBY DECLARE THAT IT IS TIME TO ENGAGE THE MORFO BALL!

MASTER KOMODO PRESENTS THE MORFO BALL TO TOMIKO...

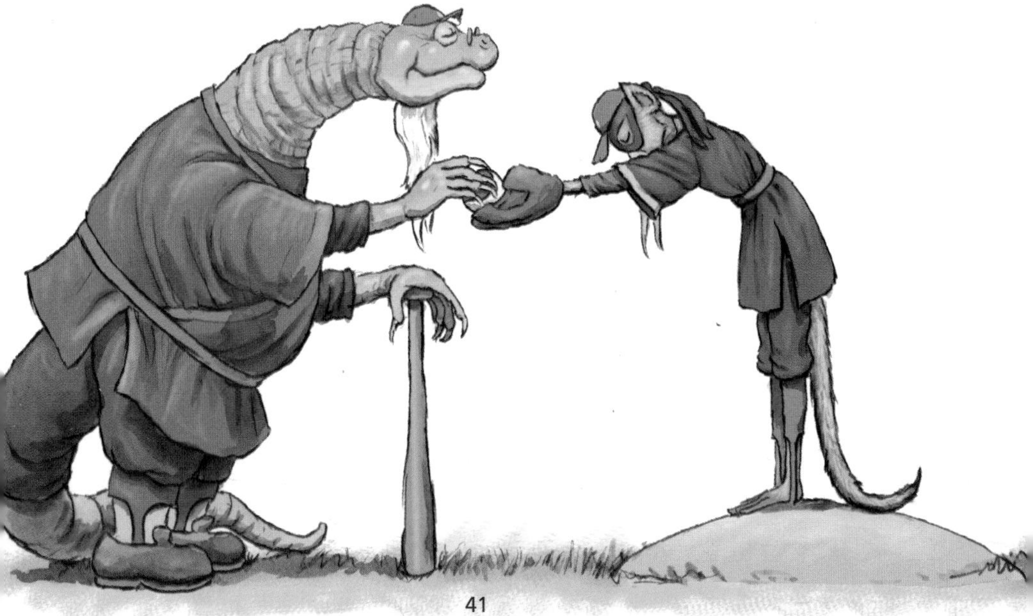

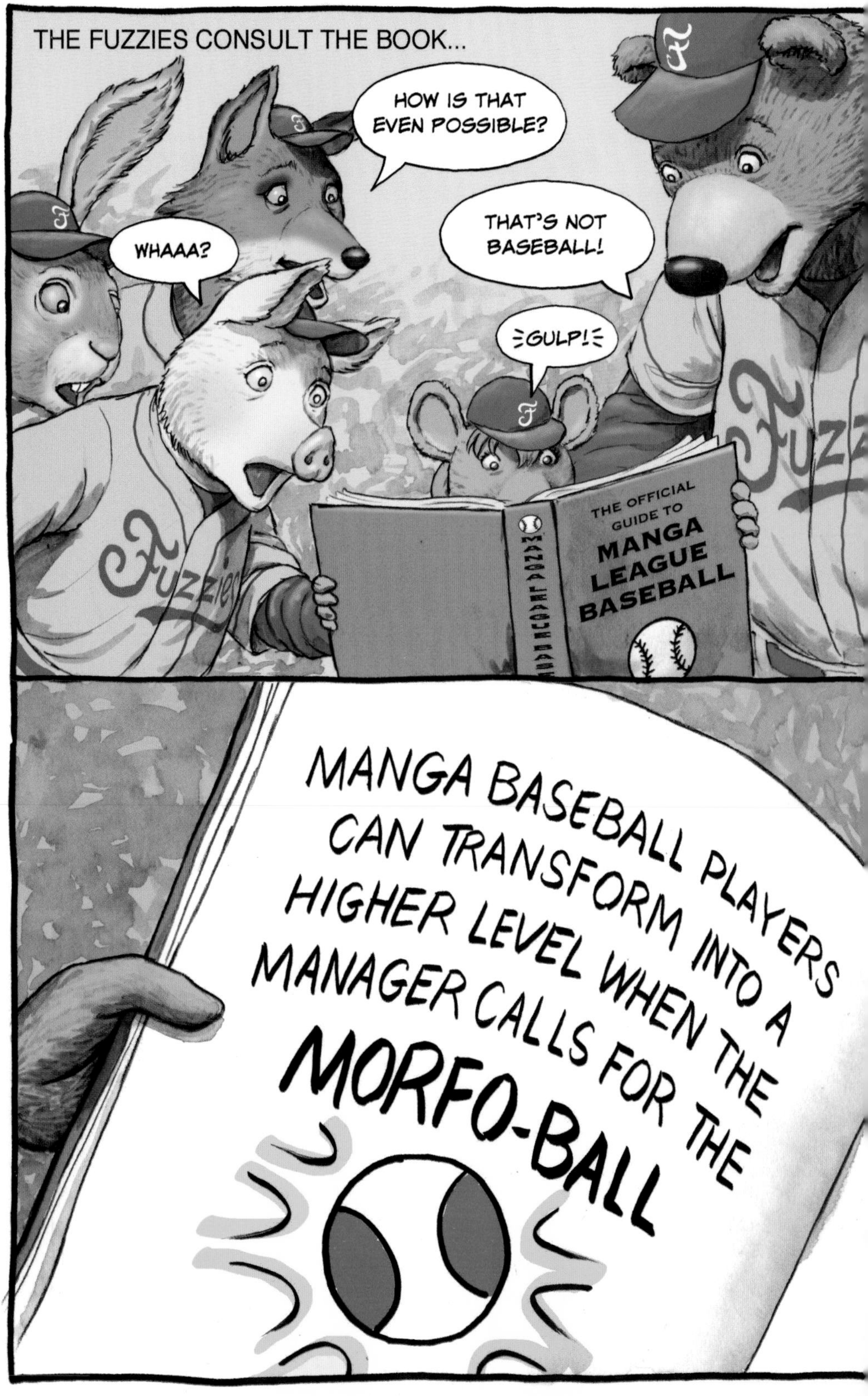
THE FUZZIES CONSULT THE BOOK...
WHAAA?
HOW IS THAT EVEN POSSIBLE?
THAT'S NOT BASEBALL!
GULP!
THE OFFICIAL GUIDE TO MANGA LEAGUE BASEBALL
MANGA LEAGUE BASEBALL
MANGA BASEBALL PLAYERS CAN TRANSFORM INTO A HIGHER LEVEL WHEN THE MANAGER CALLS FOR THE
MORFO-BALL

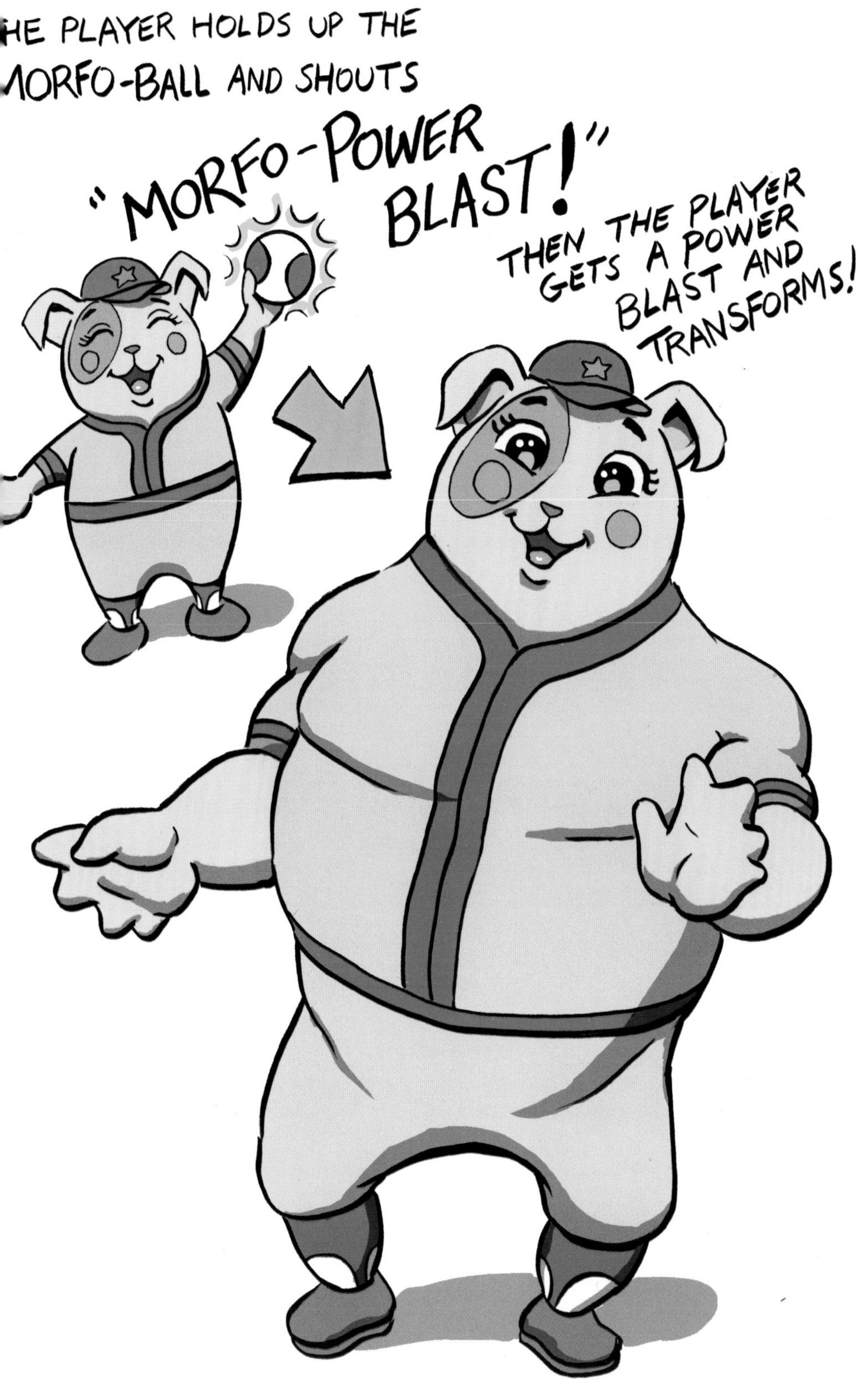
HE PLAYER HOLDS UP THE
MORFO-BALL AND SHOUTS
"MORFO-POWER BLAST!"
THEN THE PLAYER GETS A POWER BLAST AND TRANSFORMS!

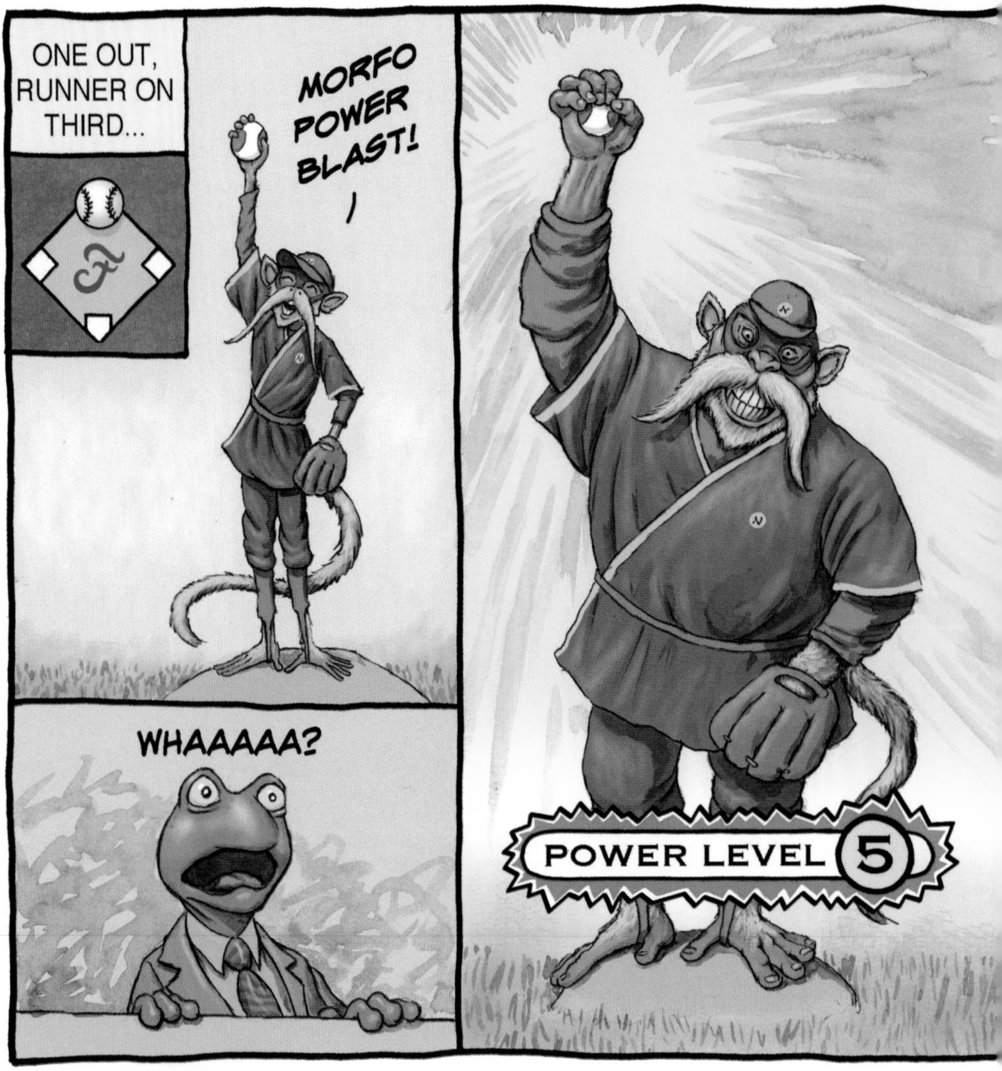
ONE OUT, RUNNER ON THIRD...
MORFO POWER BLAST!
WHAAAAA?
POWER LEVEL 5

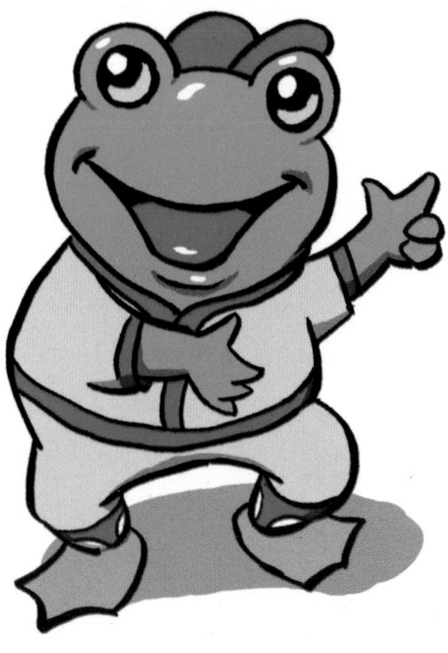

IN MANGA-BASEBALL YOUR MORFO-POWER BLAST **POWER LEVEL** IS BASED ON YOUR **PASSION FOR BASEBALL!**

ARRY AND THE NEXT BATTER STRIKE OUT TO END THE TOP OF HE SECOND INNING...

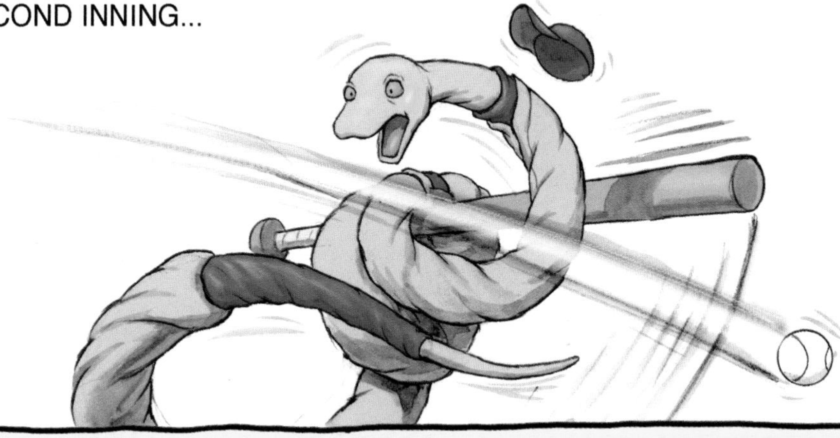

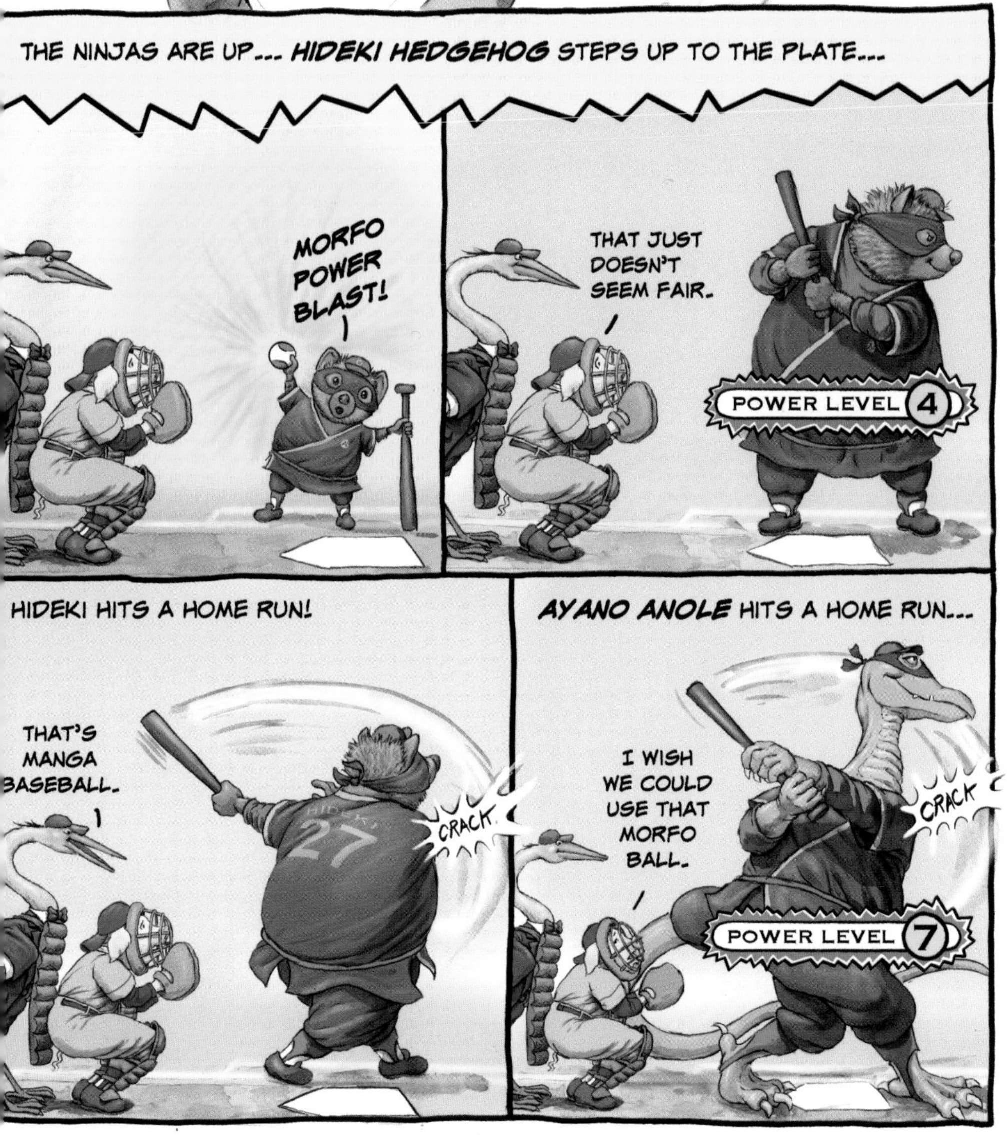
THE NINJAS ARE UP... HIDEKI HEDGEHOG STEPS UP TO THE PLATE...
MORFO POWER BLAST!
THAT JUST DOESN'T SEEM FAIR.
POWER LEVEL 4
HIDEKI HITS A HOME RUN!
THAT'S MANGA ASEBALL.
HIDEKI 27
CRACK
AYANO ANOLE HITS A HOME RUN...
I WISH WE COULD USE THAT MORFO BALL.
CRACK
POWER LEVEL 7

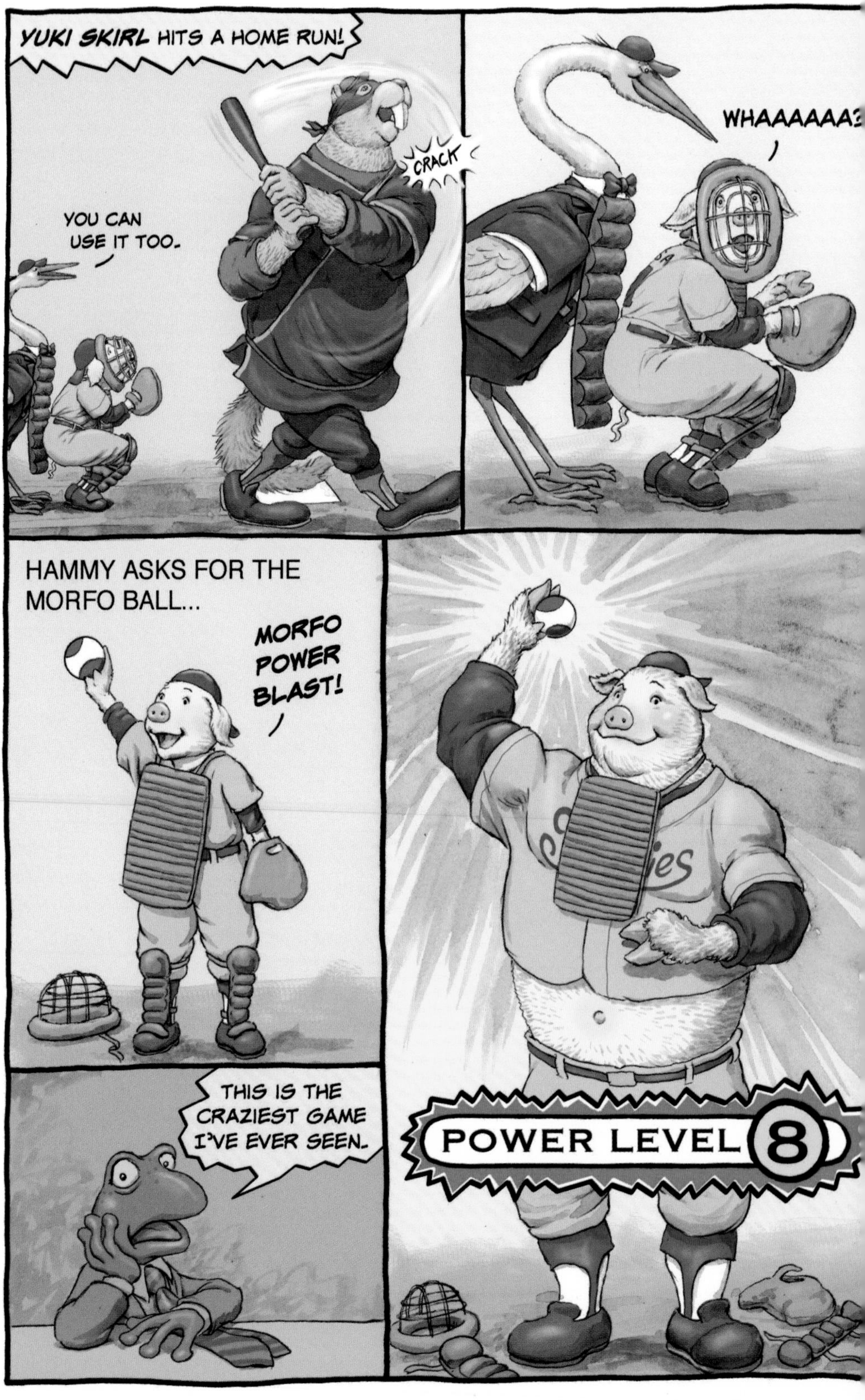

YUKI SKIRL HITS A HOME RUN!
YOU CAN USE IT TOO.
CRACK
WHAAAAAA
HAMMY ASKS FOR THE MORFO BALL...
MORFO POWER BLAST!
THIS IS THE CRAZIEST GAME I'VE EVER SEEN.
POWER LEVEL 8

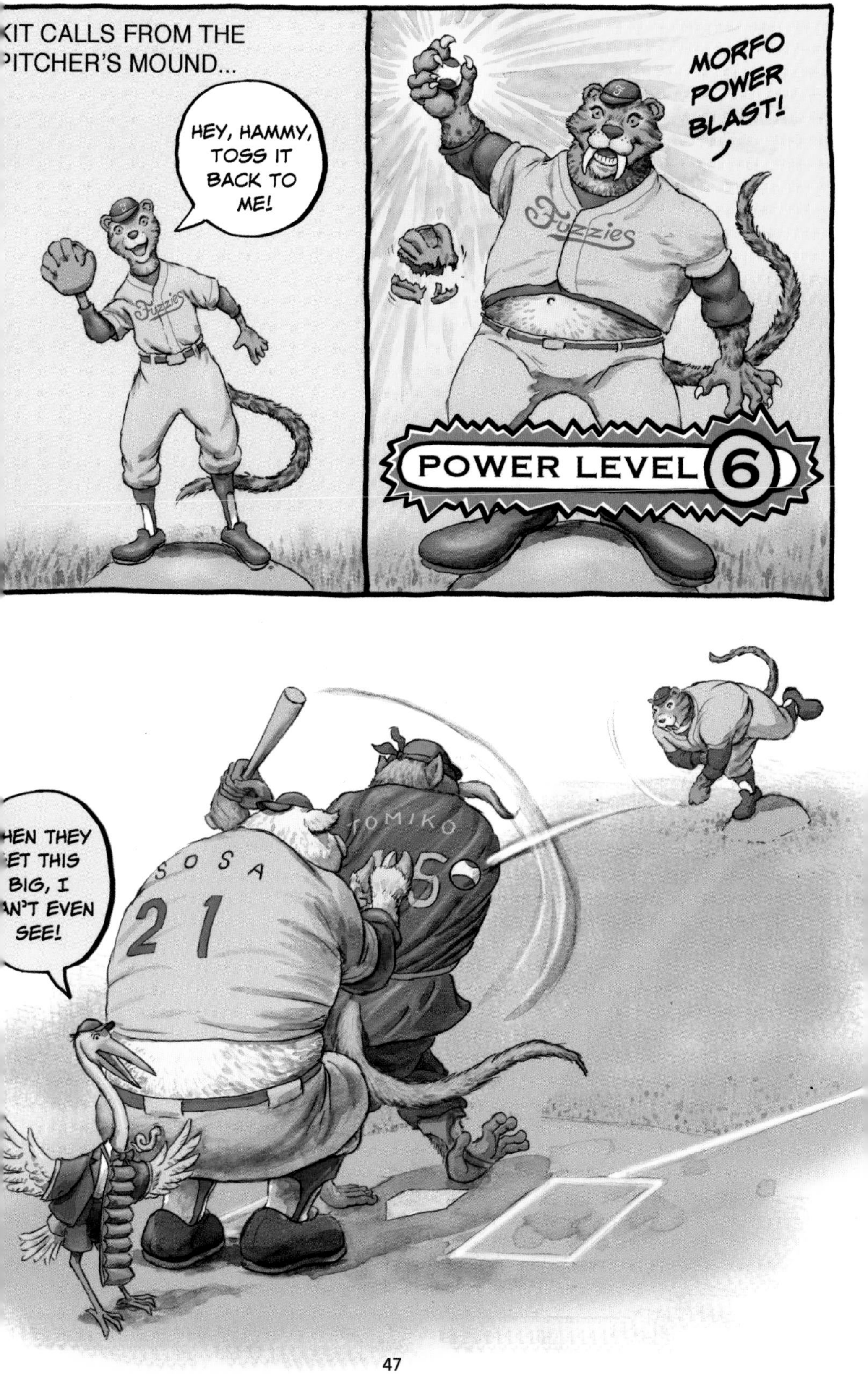
KIT CALLS FROM THE
ITCHER'S MOUND...
HEY, HAMMY, TOSS IT BACK TO ME!
Fuzzies
MORFO POWER BLAST!
Fuzzies
POWER LEVEL 6
HEN THEY ET THIS BIG, I N'T EVEN SEE!
SOSA 21
TOMIKO 5

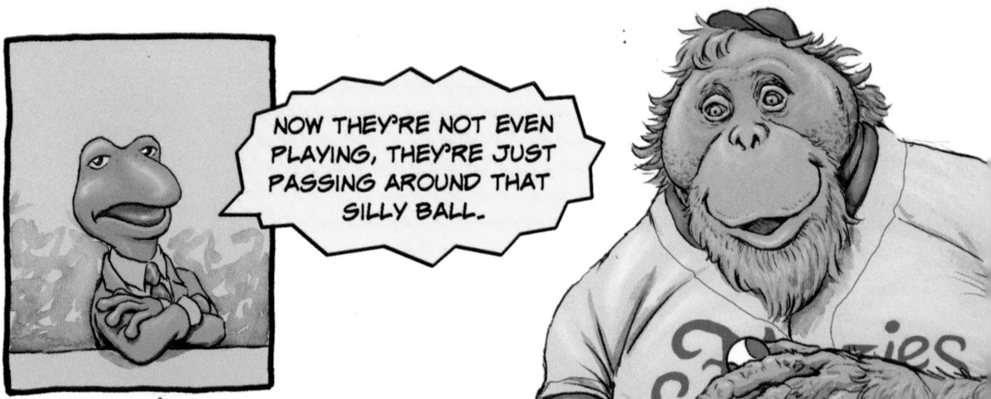
NOW THEY'RE NOT EVEN PLAYING, THEY'RE JUST PASSING AROUND THAT SILLY BALL.

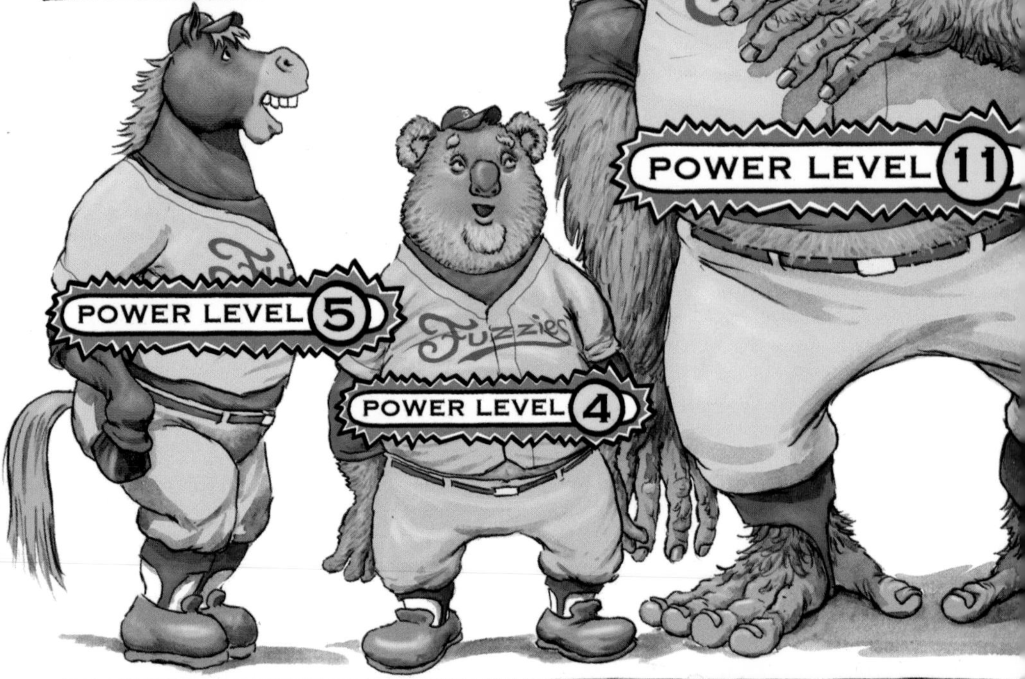
POWER LEVEL 11
POWER LEVEL 5
Fuzzies
POWER LEVEL 4

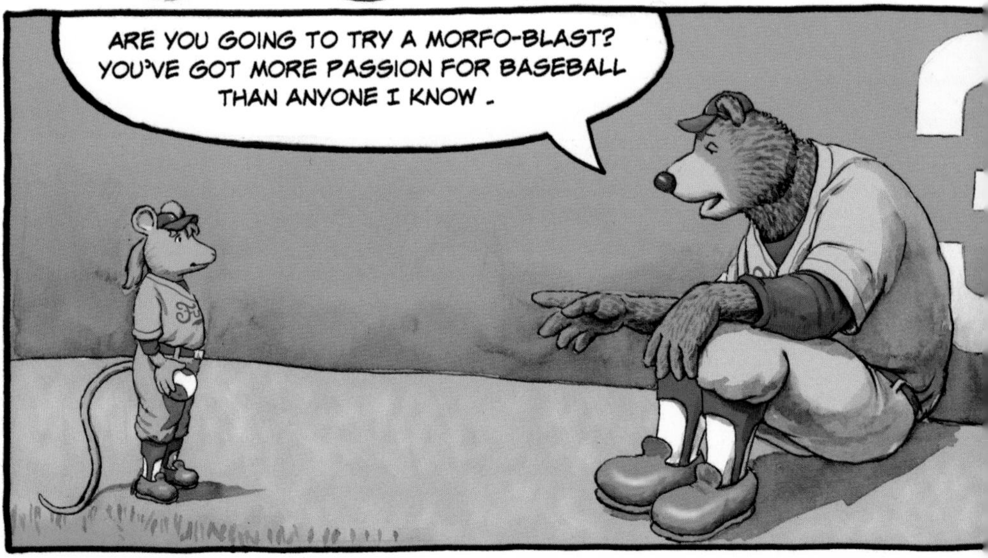
ARE YOU GOING TO TRY A MORFO-BLAST? YOU'VE GOT MORE PASSION FOR BASEBALL THAN ANYONE I KNOW.

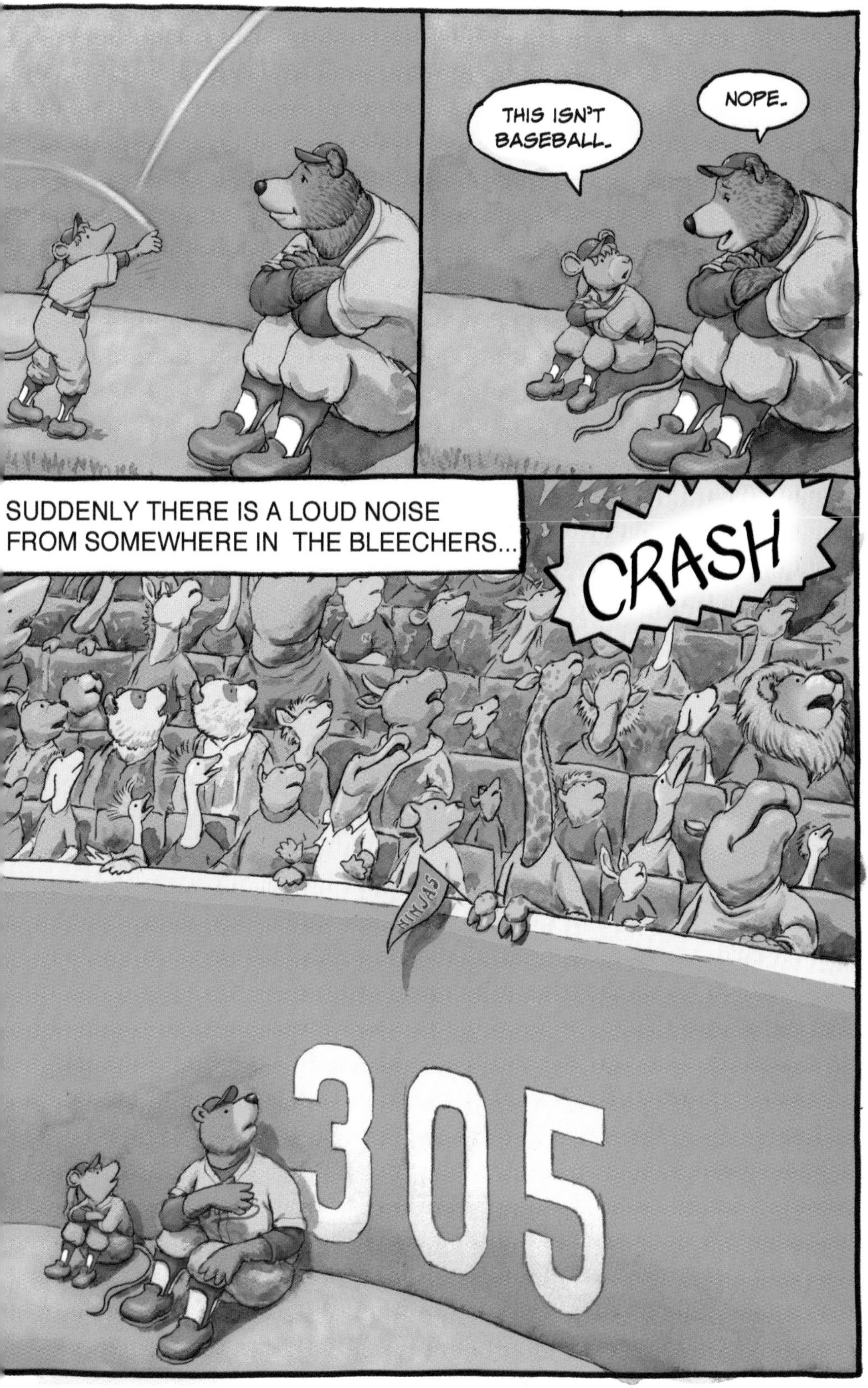
THIS ISN'T BASEBALL.
NOPE.
SUDDENLY THERE IS A LOUD NOISE FROM SOMEWHERE IN THE BLEECHERS...
CRASH
NINJAS
305

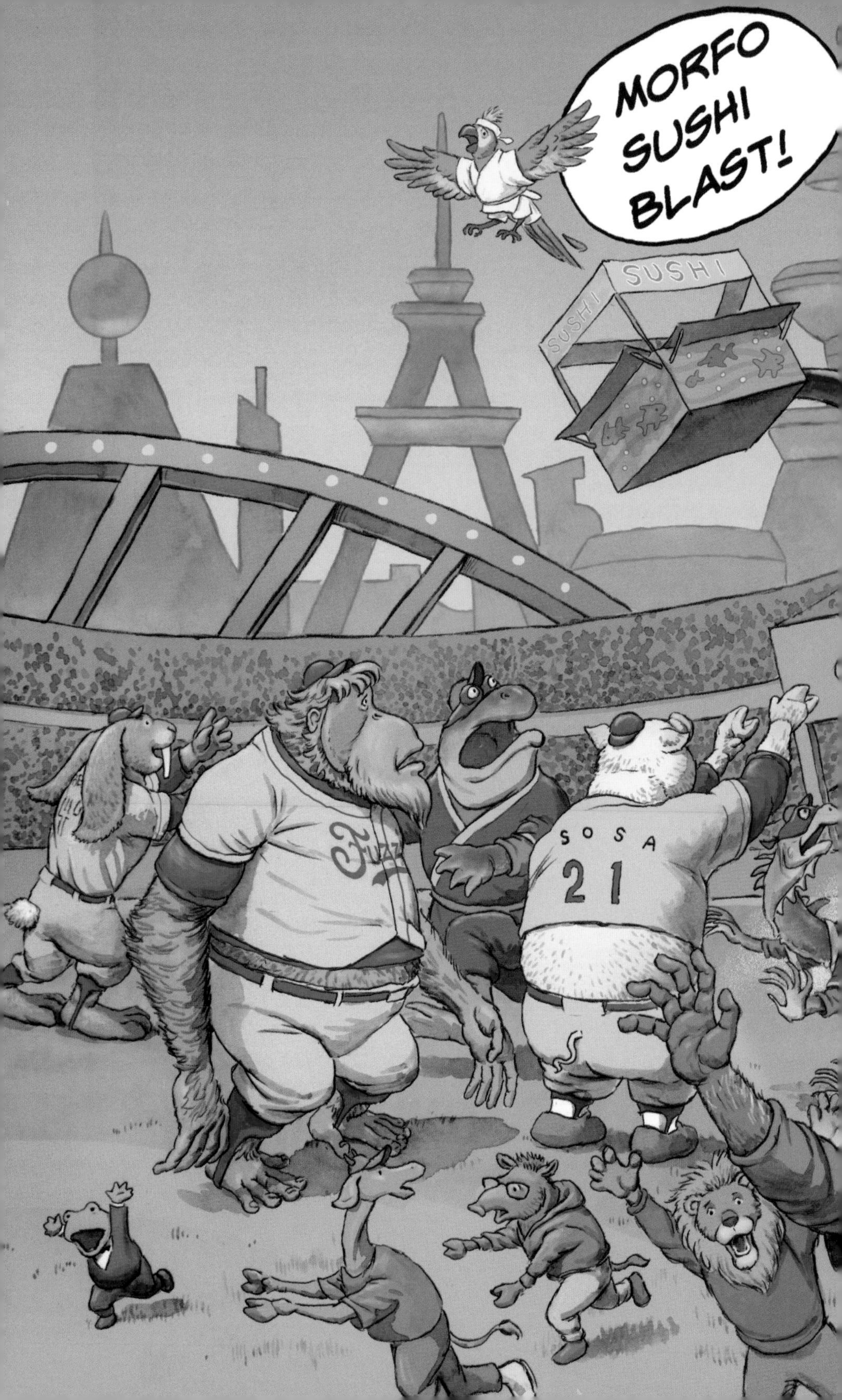
MORFO SUSHI BLAST!
SUSHI
SUSHI
SOSA
21

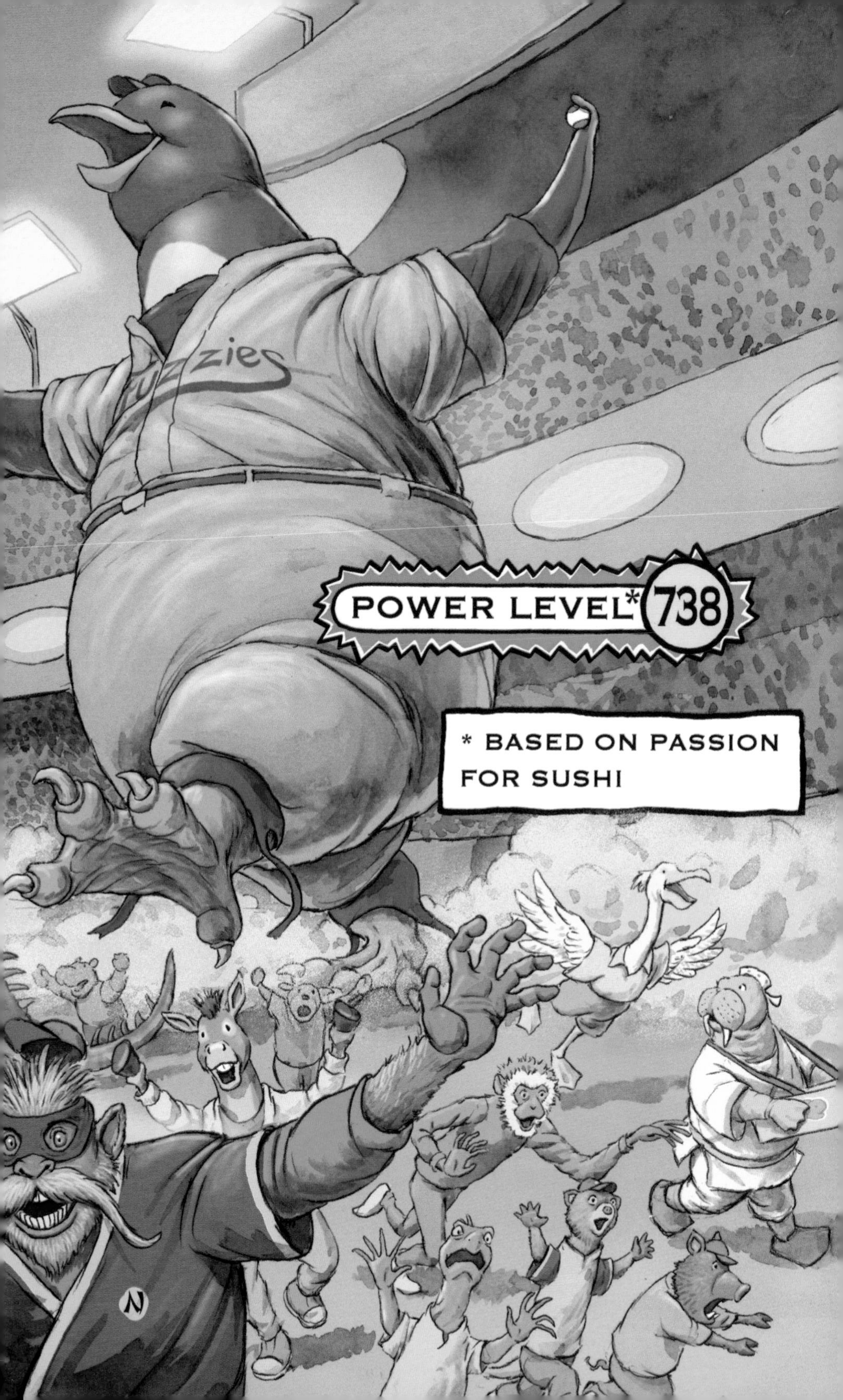

Fuzzies
POWER LEVEL* 738
* BASED ON PASSION FOR SUSHI

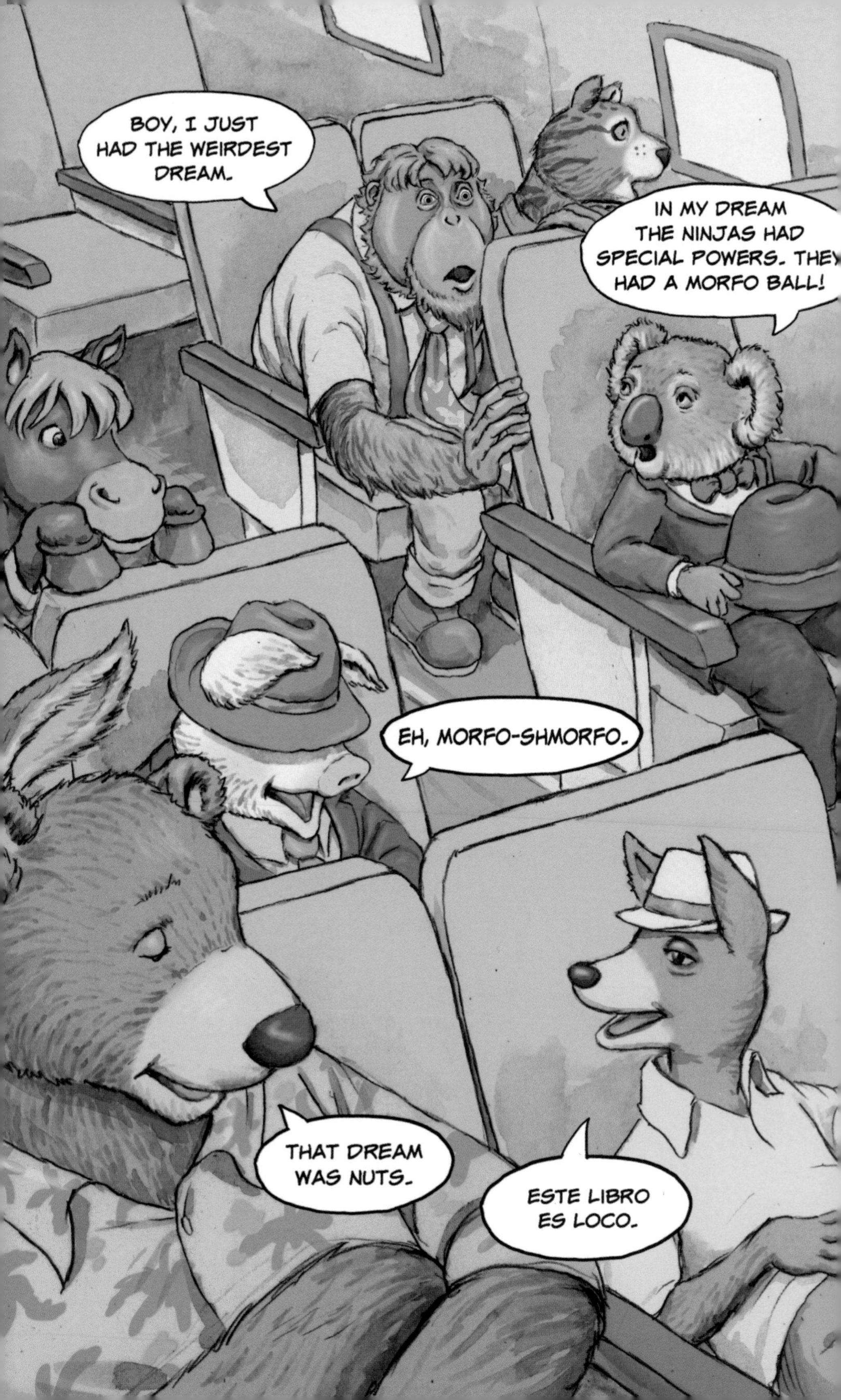
BOY, I JUST HAD THE WEIRDEST DREAM.
IN MY DREAM THE NINJAS HAD SPECIAL POWERS. THEY HAD A MORFO BALL!
EH, MORFO-SHMORFO.
THAT DREAM WAS NUTS.
ESTE LIBRO ES LOCO.

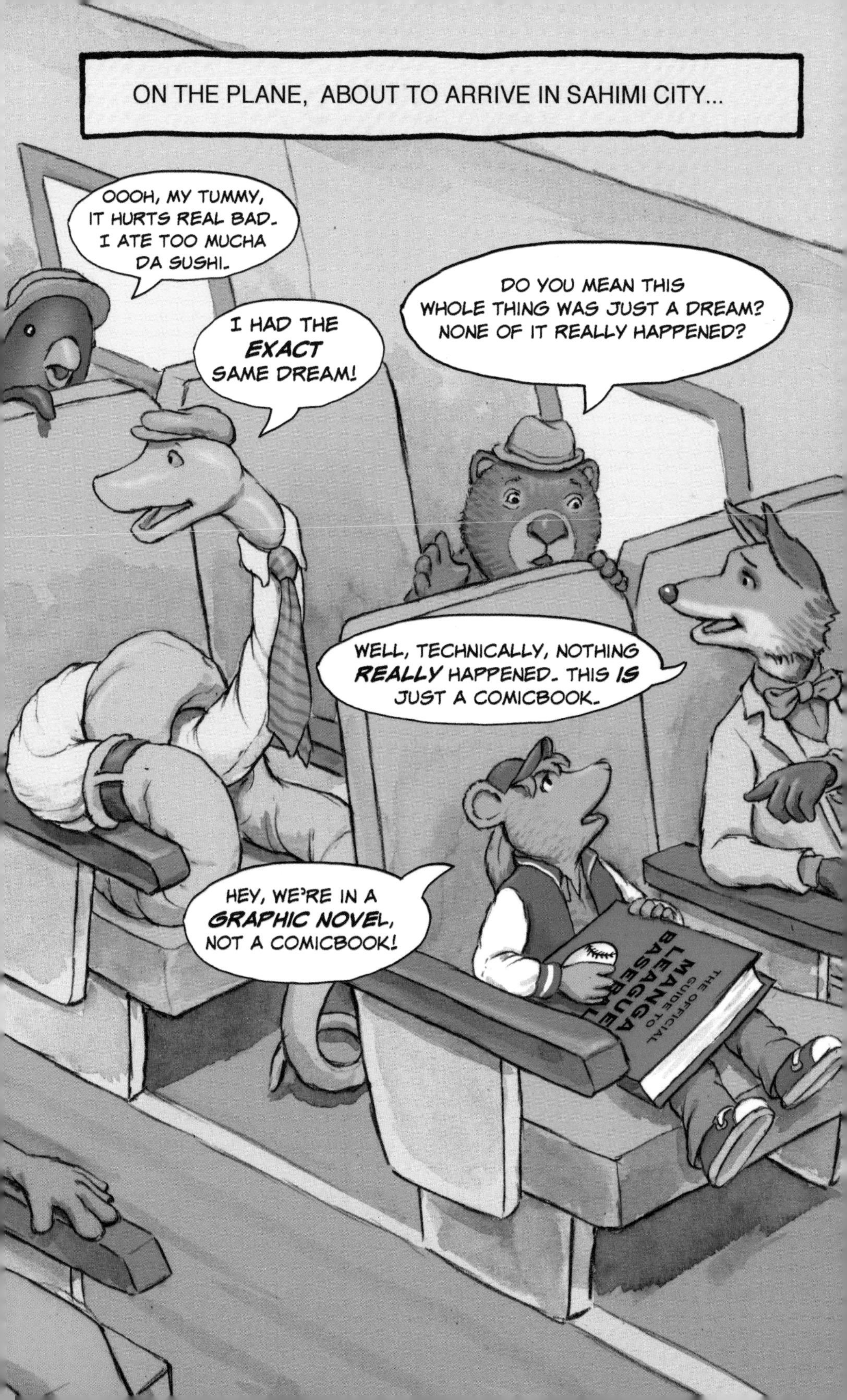
ON THE PLANE, ABOUT TO ARRIVE IN SAHIMI CITY...
OOOH, MY TUMMY, IT HURTS REAL BAD. I ATE TOO MUCHA DA SUSHI.
I HAD THE *EXACT* SAME DREAM!
DO YOU MEAN THIS WHOLE THING WAS JUST A DREAM? NONE OF IT REALLY HAPPENED?
WELL, TECHNICALLY, NOTHING *REALLY* HAPPENED. THIS *IS* JUST A COMICBOOK.
HEY, WE'RE IN A *GRAPHIC NOVEL*, NOT A COMICBOOK!
THE OFFICIAL GUIDE TO

THE END

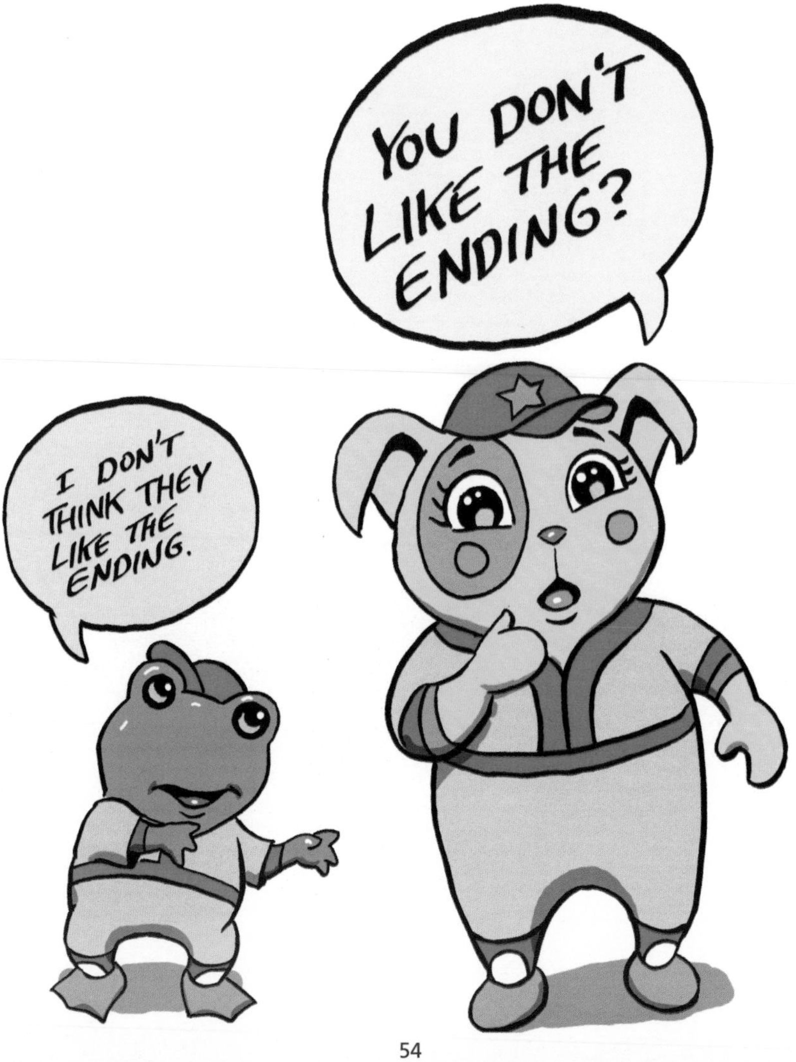
YOU DON'T LIKE THE ENDING?
I DON'T THINK THEY LIKE THE ENDING.

INSTANT REPLAY

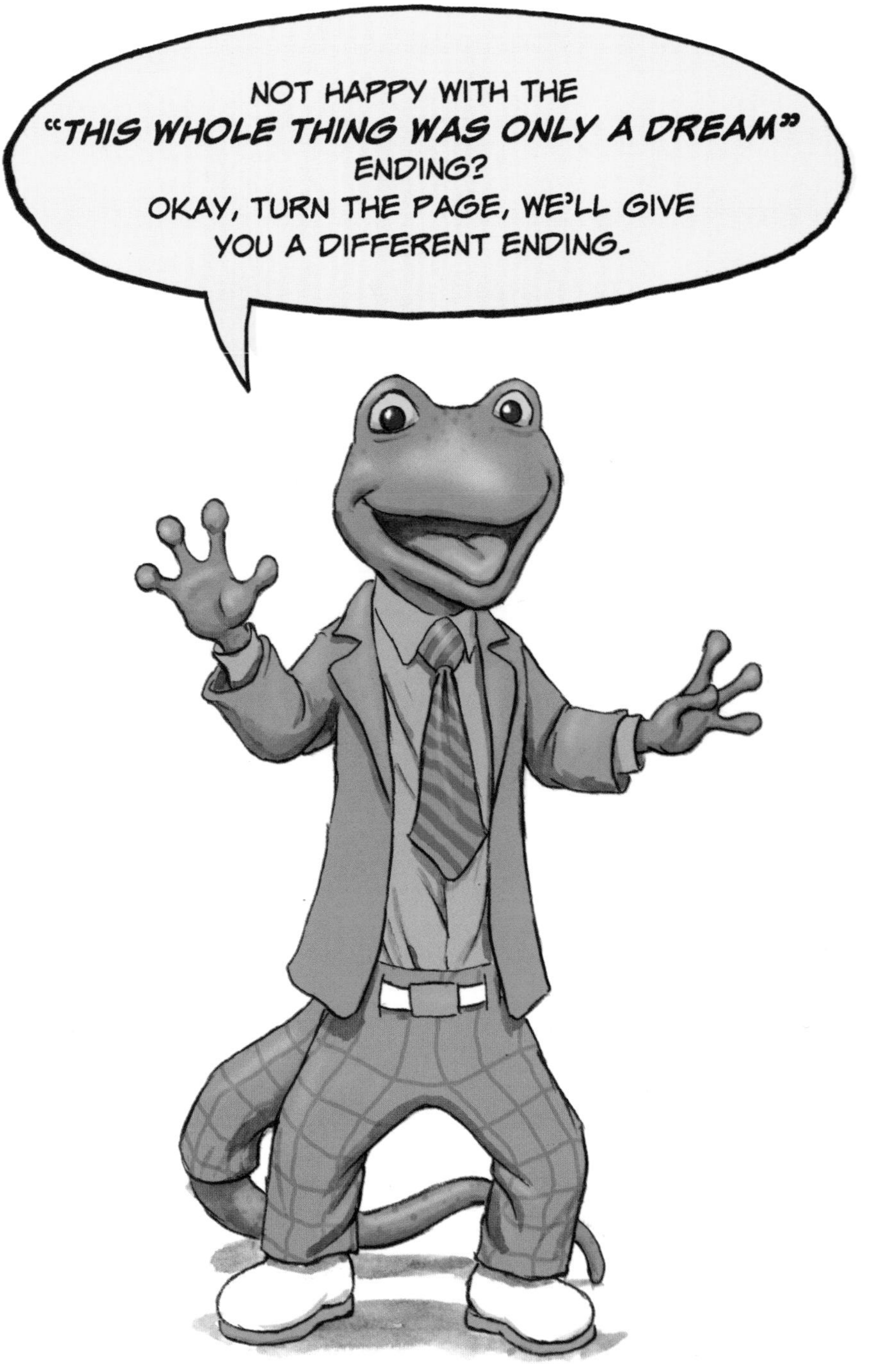
NOT HAPPY WITH THE
"*THIS WHOLE THING WAS ONLY A DREAM*"
ENDING?
OKAY, TURN THE PAGE, WE'LL GIVE
YOU A DIFFERENT ENDING.

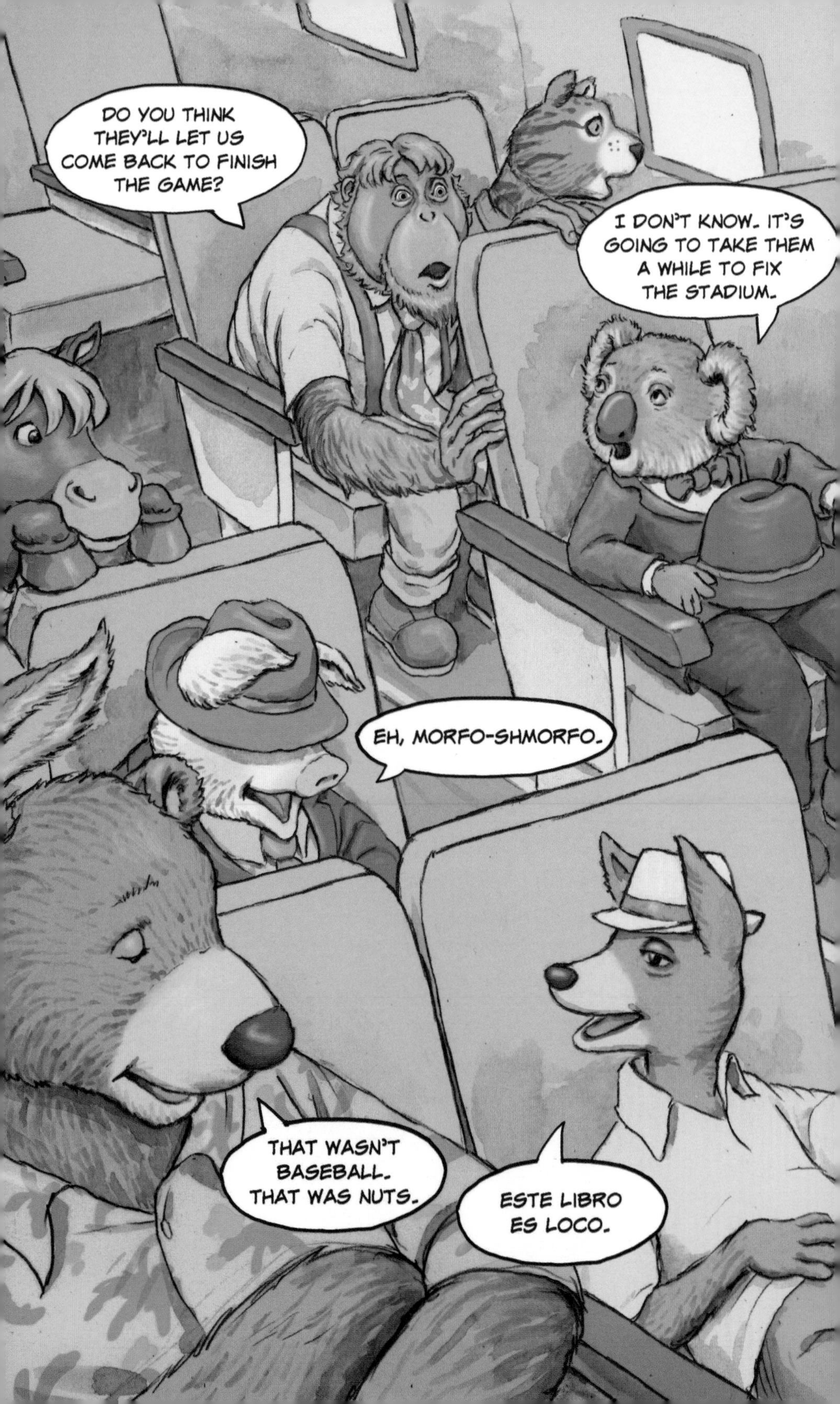
DO YOU THINK THEY'LL LET US COME BACK TO FINISH THE GAME?
I DON'T KNOW. IT'S GOING TO TAKE THEM A WHILE TO FIX THE STADIUM.
EH, MORFO-SHMORFO.
THAT WASN'T BASEBALL. THAT WAS NUTS.
ESTE LIBRO ES LOCO.

ON THE PLANE, RETURNING TO FERNWOOD VALLEY...
OOOH, MY TUMMY, IT HURTS REAL BAD. I ATE TOO MUCHA DA SUSHI.
IT WAS THEIR FAULT.
THEY SHOULD HAVE TOLD US ABOUT THE MORFO BALL.
WELL, IT WAS A SPIRITED BIT OF FUN, I SAY.
WE GOT TO SEE SASHIMI CITY, THAT WAS NICE!

A MEMO FROM THE COMMISIONER

Baseball was introduced to Japan from America around 1870. In "Ninja Baseball Blast" I wanted to celebrate many of the fun things that our culture has imported from Japan. The Fuzzies meet ninjas, try sushi, learn from a manga style textbook, and even encounter a giant kaiju (Godzila is an example of a famous kaiju).

I also wanted to have some fun with the idea of transformation. In Japanese influenced shows, cars transform into giant robots, rangers morph into mighty warriors, and little pocket monsters evolve into larger pocket monsters. In English literature, Alice goes through many transformations in Wonderland, and Dr. Jekyll transforms into Mr. Hyde. In American movies, people transform into werewolves and superheroes all the time. Even Bugs Bunny transforms (when he meets Dr. Jekyll).

As a child, my drawing style was influenced by cartoons created by Walt Disney and Warner Bros. Today, the drawing style of American school children is often influenced by Japanese comics which were created by Japanese artists who grew up watching those same American cartoons (among so many other influences as well). It's amazing the way a culture can absorb an influence from across the globe and transform it into something unique.

I hope you enjoyed reading about the Fuzzies' wacky, and transformative, encounter with another culture.

John Steven Gurney

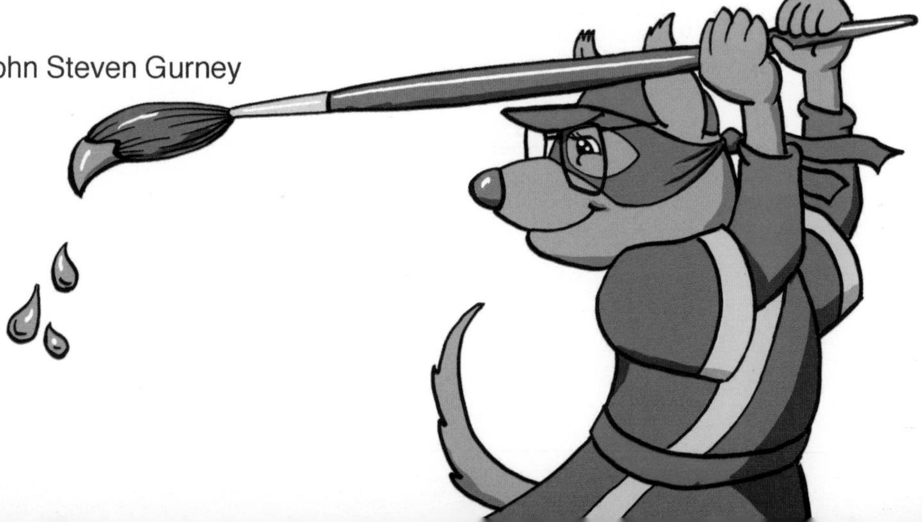

WATCH OUT FOR PAPERCUTZ™

Even though FUZZY BASEBALL #1 was clearly a homerun, we're just now making it to second! The second FUZZY BASEBALL graphic novel, that is. Welcome to the second, screwball FUZZY BASEBALL graphic novel, by John Steven Gurney (learn more about the talented Mr. Gurney at johnstevengurney.com), from Papercutz, those FUZZY BASEBALL season ticket holders dedicated to publishing great graphic novels for all ages. I'm Jim Salicrup, Editor-in-Chief and Technical Error collector.

In "Ninja Baseball Blast," we see the Fernwood Valley Fuzzies battle the Sashimi City Ninjas, and as exciting as that classic encounter turned out, now I'm wondering what games against other Papercutz superstars would be like. For example, the Fuzzies would have a great advantage playing against THE SMURFS. After all, the Smurfs are only three apples, or baseballs, tall. Probably the only Smurf able to lift a regulation-size bat would be Hefty Smurf. Unless Papa Smurf came up with some kind of magical spell, I'm betting the Fuzzies would clobber the Smurfs.

On the other baseball-gloved hand, Lincoln Loud and his ten sisters, Lori, Leni, Luna, Luan, Lynn, Lucy, Lola, Lana, Lisa, and Lily, the stars of the hit Nickelodeon TV series THE LOUD HOUSE and of their own Papercutz graphic novel series, stand a much better chance against the Fuzzies. The Fuzzies would probably still easily win, they are a real baseball team, after all, but I wouldn't underestimate Lynn Loud's sports skills and ability to whip her team into shape—she has more than enough siblings to put together an all-Loud line-up, although Lily may be a little too young to play.

A much tougher team might be made up from the stars of THE ONLY LIVING GIRL (The exciting follow-up graphic novel series to THE ONLY LIVING BOY). With just two human players, Zee and Erik, and a bunch of mutants and monsters, this team will pack a wallop, if not a lot of finesse. If Erik can swing a bat as well as he does his wooden sword or if Morgan Dwar focused her considerable combat skills, they could possibly pull off a surprise upset.

Another power-hitting dream team could be composed of the combined casts from MANOSAURS and DINOSAUR EXPLORERS. Just imagine a team with humans, dinosaurs, and human/dinosaur hybrids! While some of the dinosaurs may not grasp the concept of baseball, how could you not want a real-life raptor on your team? How DINOSAUR EXPLORERS' Rain, Emily, Sean, and Stone would get along with MANOSAURS' Tri, Rex, Ptor, and Pterry is another story. (Check out the preview of DINOSAUR EXPLORERS #1 on the following pages, if you haven't picked up their great graphic novels yet!)

But the team I'm probably most excited about is the gang from THE HOTEL TRANSYLVANIA (the stars of the hit movies, animated TV series, and Papercutz graphic novels)! This would definitely be loads of fun to watch. Not necessarily to witness a well-played game, but just to see how wild and wacky things would get. THE HOTEL TRANSYLVANIA would even have three players (Mavis, Drac, and Vlad) that can literally turn into bats. Not baseball bats, but bats! And who could possibly steal bases better than the Invisible Man?

Who knows what really awaits the Fernwood Fuzzies next? Who could've guessed they'd play against ninjas? Probably John Steven Gurney knows, but he's not telling. We'll just have to wait for the next FUZZY BASEBALL graphic novel to find out.

Thanks,

Jim

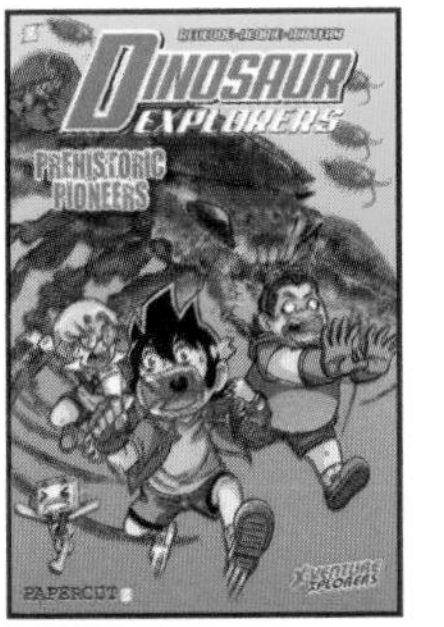
DINOSAUR EXPLORERS
PREHISTORIC PIONEERS
PAPERCUTZ

© 2011 KADOKAWA GEMPAK STARZ.

STAY IN TOUCH!

EMAIL:	salicrup@papercutz.com
WEB:	papercutz.com
TWITTER:	@papercutzgn
INSTAGRAM:	@papercutzgn
FACEBOOK:	PAPERCUTZGRAPHICNOVELS
REGULAR MAIL:	Papercutz, 160 Broadway, Suite 700, East Wing, New York, NY 10038

Here's a special preview of DINOSAUR EXPLORERS #1 "Prehistoric Pioneers"...

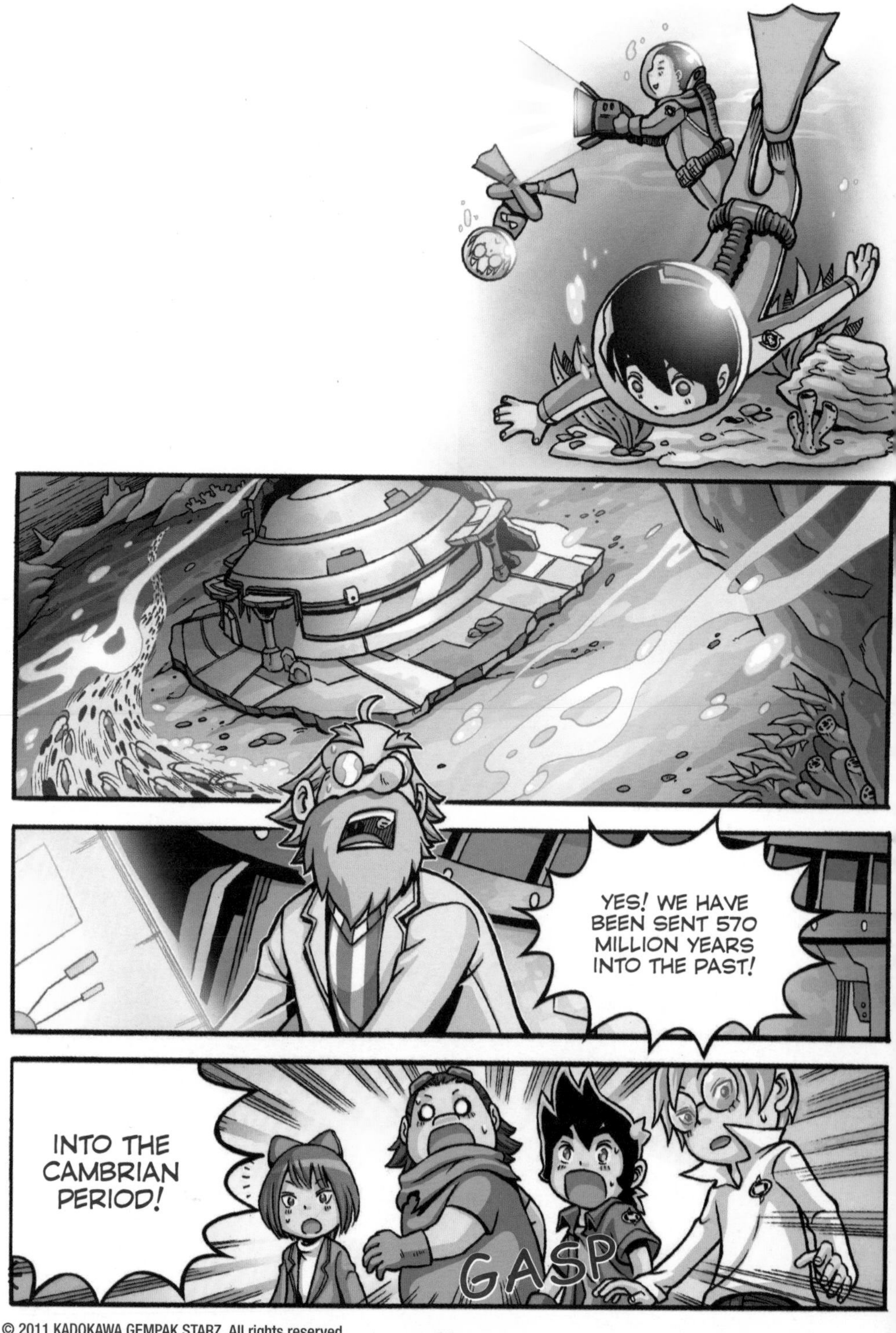
YES! WE HAVE BEEN SENT 570 MILLION YEARS INTO THE PAST!
INTO THE CAMBRIAN PERIOD!
GASP

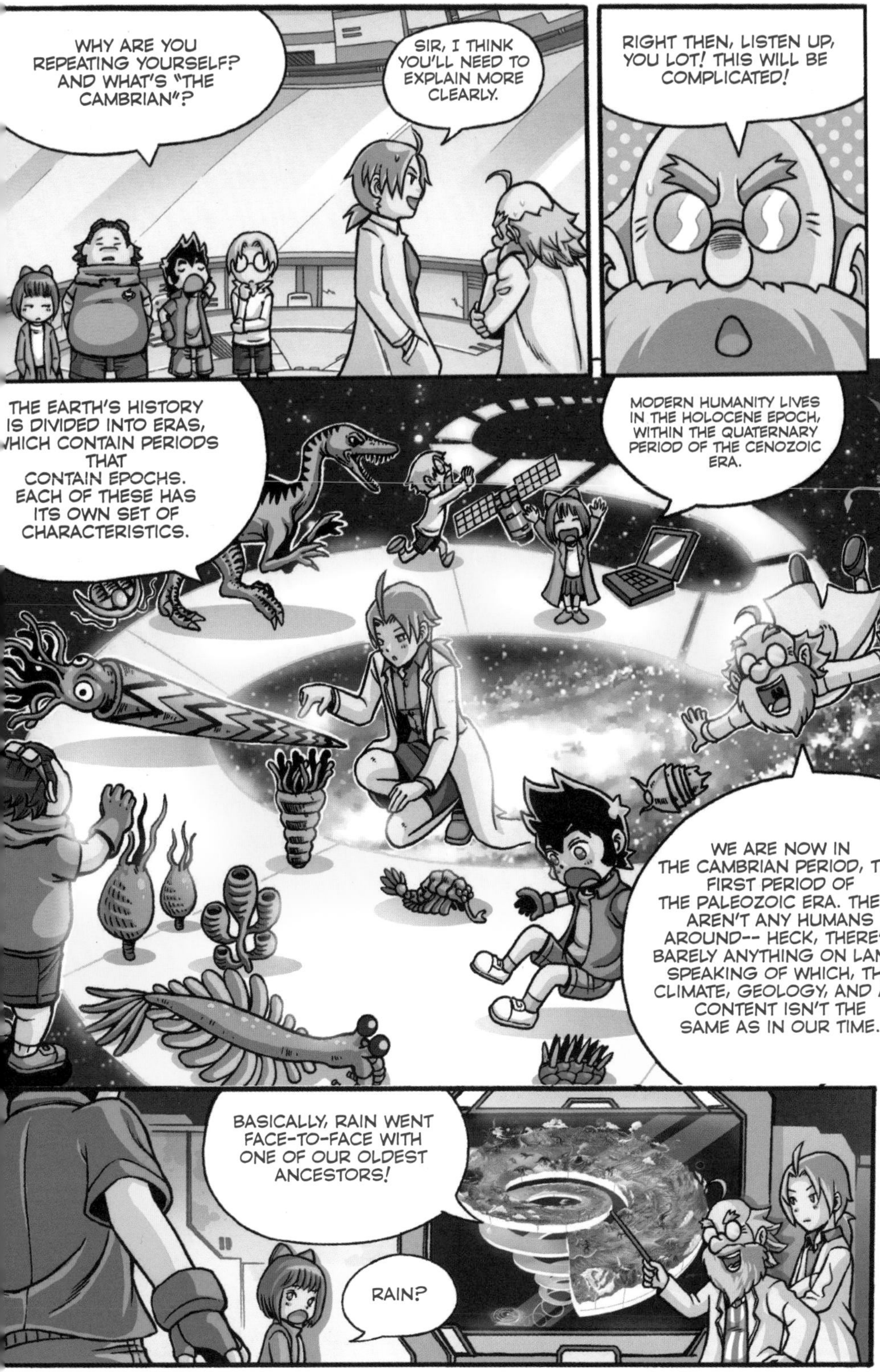
WHY ARE YOU REPEATING YOURSELF? AND WHAT'S "THE CAMBRIAN"?
SIR, I THINK YOU'LL NEED TO EXPLAIN MORE CLEARLY.
RIGHT THEN, LISTEN UP, YOU LOT! THIS WILL BE COMPLICATED!
THE EARTH'S HISTORY IS DIVIDED INTO ERAS, WHICH CONTAIN PERIODS THAT CONTAIN EPOCHS. EACH OF THESE HAS ITS OWN SET OF CHARACTERISTICS.
MODERN HUMANITY LIVES IN THE HOLOCENE EPOCH, WITHIN THE QUATERNARY PERIOD OF THE CENOZOIC ERA.
WE ARE NOW IN THE CAMBRIAN PERIOD, THE FIRST PERIOD OF THE PALEOZOIC ERA. THERE AREN'T ANY HUMANS AROUND-- HECK, THERE'S BARELY ANYTHING ON LAND! SPEAKING OF WHICH, THE CLIMATE, GEOLOGY, AND AIR CONTENT ISN'T THE SAME AS IN OUR TIME.
BASICALLY, RAIN WENT FACE-TO-FACE WITH ONE OF OUR OLDEST ANCESTORS!
RAIN?

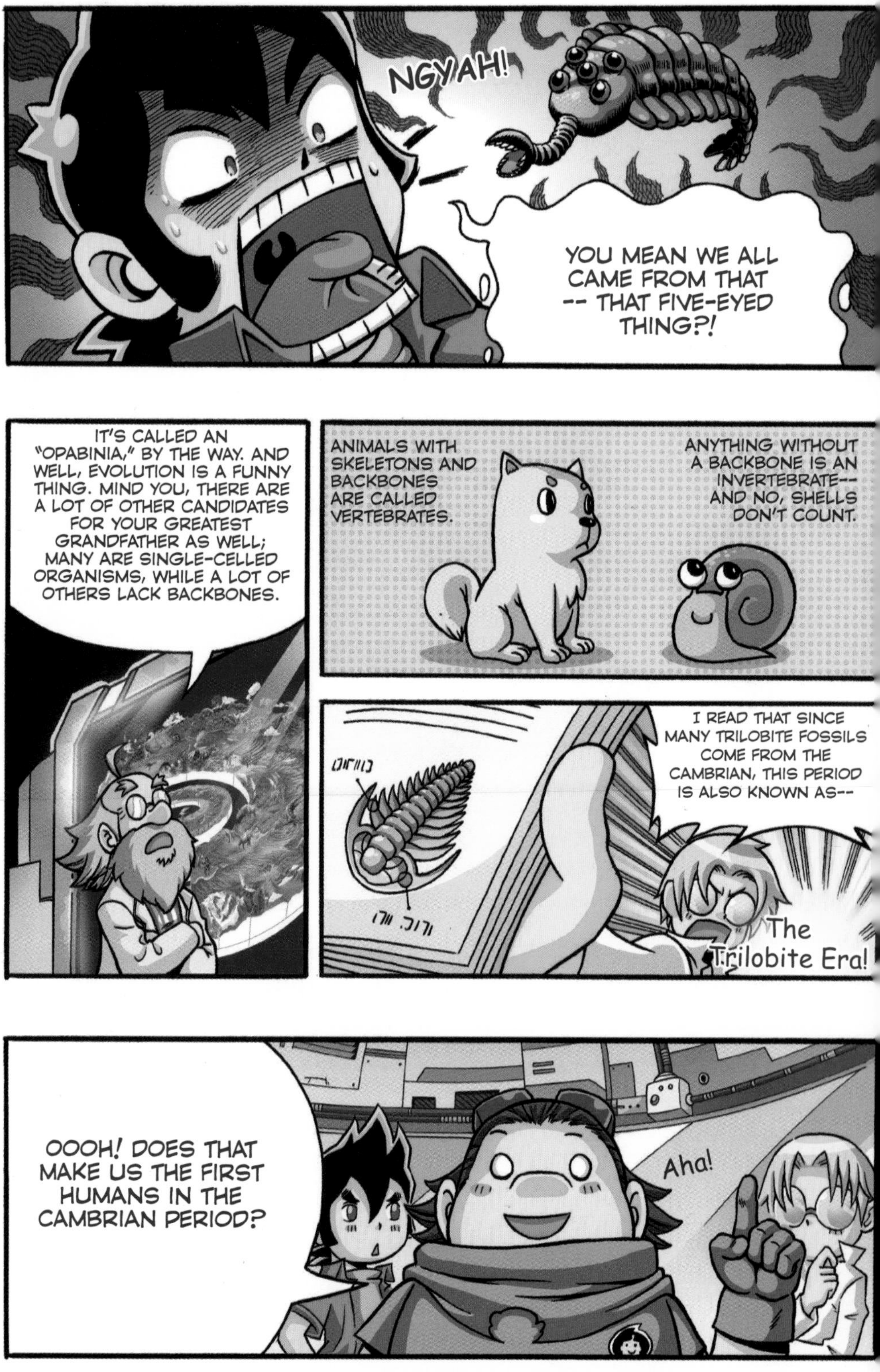
NGYAH!
YOU MEAN WE ALL CAME FROM THAT -- THAT FIVE-EYED THING?!
IT'S CALLED AN "OPABINIA," BY THE WAY. AND WELL, EVOLUTION IS A FUNNY THING. MIND YOU, THERE ARE A LOT OF OTHER CANDIDATES FOR YOUR GREATEST GRANDFATHER AS WELL; MANY ARE SINGLE-CELLED ORGANISMS, WHILE A LOT OF OTHERS LACK BACKBONES.
ANIMALS WITH SKELETONS AND BACKBONES ARE CALLED VERTEBRATES.
ANYTHING WITHOUT A BACKBONE IS AN INVERTEBRATE-- AND NO, SHELLS DON'T COUNT.
I READ THAT SINCE MANY TRILOBITE FOSSILS COME FROM THE CAMBRIAN, THIS PERIOD IS ALSO KNOWN AS--
The Trilobite Era!
OOOH! DOES THAT MAKE US THE FIRST HUMANS IN THE CAMBRIAN PERIOD?
Aha!

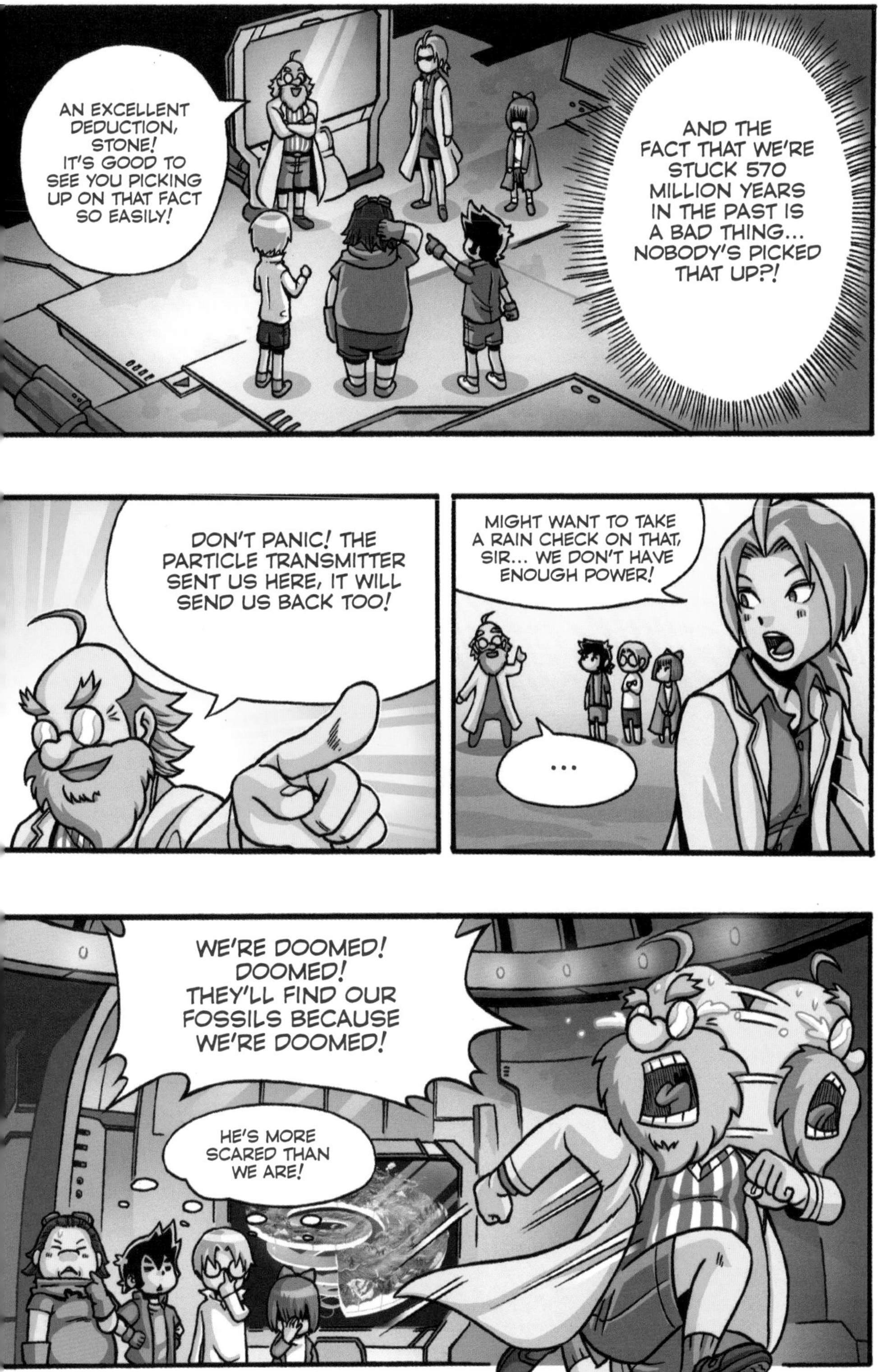
AN EXCELLENT DEDUCTION, STONE! IT'S GOOD TO SEE YOU PICKING UP ON THAT FACT SO EASILY!
AND THE FACT THAT WE'RE STUCK 570 MILLION YEARS IN THE PAST IS A BAD THING... NOBODY'S PICKED THAT UP?!
DON'T PANIC! THE PARTICLE TRANSMITTER SENT US HERE, IT WILL SEND US BACK TOO!
MIGHT WANT TO TAKE A RAIN CHECK ON THAT, SIR... WE DON'T HAVE ENOUGH POWER!
...
WE'RE DOOMED! DOOMED! THEY'LL FIND OUR FOSSILS BECAUSE WE'RE DOOMED!
HE'S MORE SCARED THAN WE ARE!

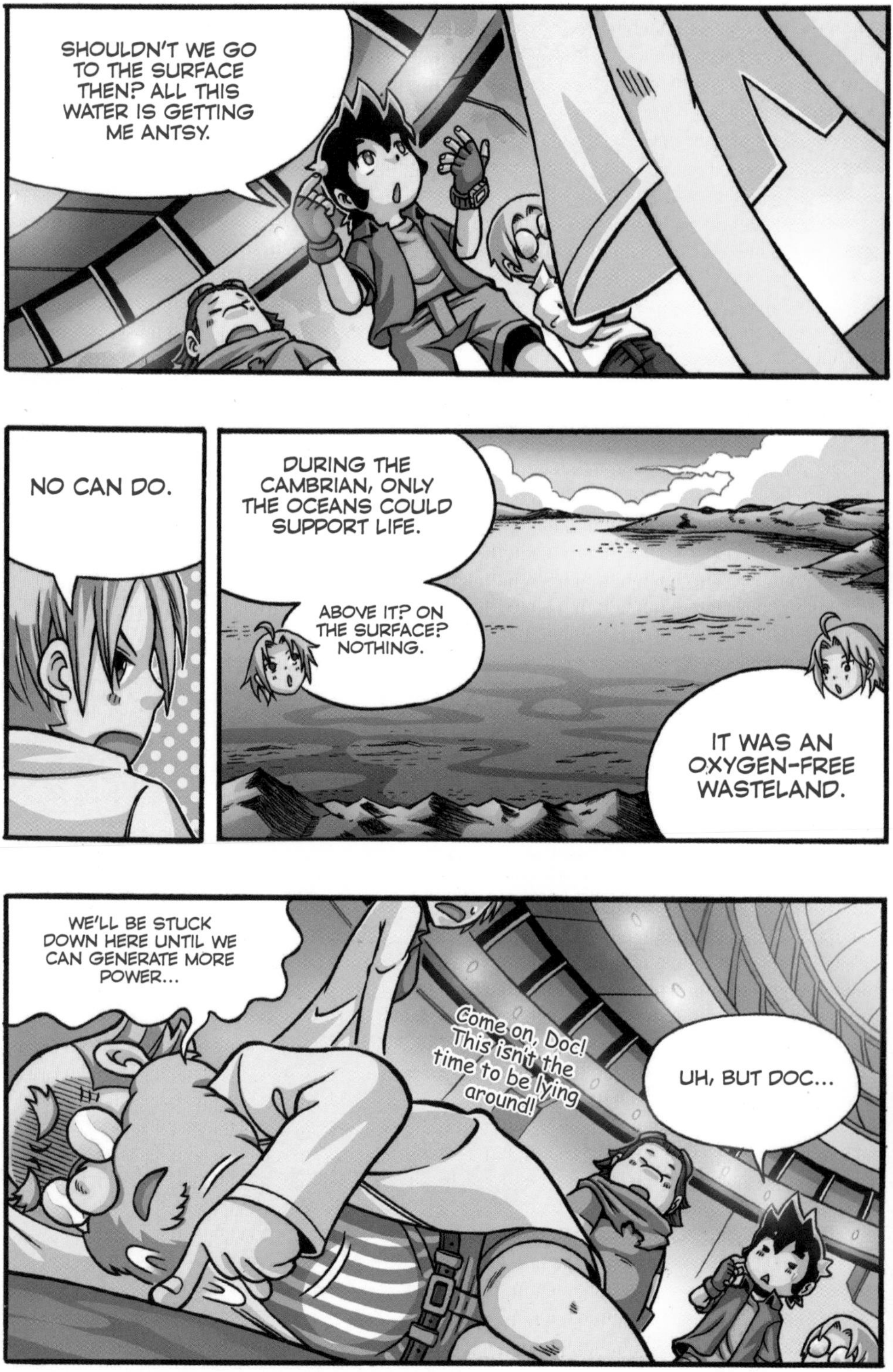
SHOULDN'T WE GO TO THE SURFACE THEN? ALL THIS WATER IS GETTING ME ANTSY.
NO CAN DO.
DURING THE CAMBRIAN, ONLY THE OCEANS COULD SUPPORT LIFE.
ABOVE IT? ON THE SURFACE? NOTHING.
IT WAS AN OXYGEN-FREE WASTELAND.
WE'LL BE STUCK DOWN HERE UNTIL WE CAN GENERATE MORE POWER...
Come on, Doc! This isn't the time to be lying around!
UH, BUT DOC...